CW00496150

The Casebook of
Holmes' Neighbour

ISBN: 9798388658074

For my mum, Madeline.

Table of Contents

A Word from the Author 5

Prologue 7

Chapter 1: Arrival in Baker Street 16

Chapter 2: The Disappointing Detective 24

Chapter 3: The Savoy Bomb Plot 37

Chapter 4: The Horse Owners' Peril 50

Chapter 5: The Case of the Rival Inventors 70

Chapter 6: The Riddle of the Vanished Viscount 91

Chapter 6: The Disappearance of Mycroft Holmes 107

Chapter 7: The Duchess's Dilemma 121

Chapter 8: The Phantom Stagecoach 135

Chapter 8: The (Mis)Adventure of the Duplicitous Diplomat
.... 151

Chapter 9: The Case of the Secret Order 167

Epilogue 212

A Word from the Author

If you're a faithful, ardent fan of Sherlock Holmes literature, *this book might not be for you*. Let me explain.

I am a true fan of Holmes mysteries; I believe I have read every single novel, novella and short story published about this amazing fictional character, canonical and otherwise. But like every human being and fictional character that has ever existed, Holmes *must* have had faults and character flaws, beyond his habit of the *7% solution*. This got me thinking: what if Sherlock Holmes was not as brilliant as Watson's stories in *The Strand* make him out to be? And what if those character flaws were so amplified, that he was inept?

This idea tumbled in my brain for a *long time*. I toyed with the idea that it was his loyal companion, Dr John Watson, that possessed the brains of the duo, modestly placing himself in his stories as merely a sidekick and Boswell. But that felt too easy and convenient.

An idea struck me that persisted and resonated over time. That being of a 'hidden hand' that guided both Holmes and Watson along a meandering path towards justice. This idea developed in my imagination over time, until eventually, a story began to take shape in my head.

Enough became enough, so I began to *intuitively* pen the narrative from my brain that was bursting to come out. I set out to develop the story and make it coherent. The delete button on my laptop being my favoured key. After many attempts, in fits and starts, one chapter became two, becoming a handful. After what seemed an age, my manuscript was ready. This book is the product of that process.

Thank you for giving me an opportunity to offer a different perspective on a tried and tested formula, and if you are a fan of

Holmes that has an intolerance for diversion from the original texts, all I can ask is *give this book a chance*. If you hate it, I offer you an apology. But if you, like me, can withstand a considerable variance from the OG Holmes character, then I hope you enjoy my work!

Prologue

My story starts long before I became neighbours with a Mr Sherlock Holmes. In the bustling metropolis of London, I, Horatio Ollerenthorpe, entered this world with neither name nor fortune to call my own. Born into abject poverty, I was but a tiny speck amidst a sea of lost souls, struggling to stay afloat amidst the filth and squalor that engulfed the city's underbelly. My earliest memories are of begging for scraps in the dark, narrow alleyways, my tiny hands outstretched in a desperate plea for sustenance. As I grew, I became acutely aware of the crushing weight of the city's indifference, the endless battle for survival that each new dawn brought.

With no family to speak of, I forged alliances with other street urchins like myself, our shared plight forging bonds of camaraderie and loyalty that would last a lifetime. Together, we formed a ragtag band of scavengers, scouring the city's darkest corners for any shred of comestible or shelter that might alleviate our abject misery. At times, we were forced to resort to thievery, our nimble fingers pilfering the pockets of unsuspecting passers-by, driven by the gnawing hunger that consumed our every waking moment.

However, I was determined to rise above the wretched circumstances of my birth, the tattered remnants of my spirit ignited by an insatiable thirst for knowledge and self-improvement. I taught myself to read and write, piecing together fragments of discarded newspapers and pilfered books, my eager mind soaking up the words like a parched sponge. And with each new word, each fresh insight into the world beyond the squalid confines of my existence, I vowed to one day escape the suffocating grasp of poverty and carve a better life for myself.

As the years passed, fate smiled upon me in the form of an itinerant troupe of street performers, their colourful costumes and lively performances a stark contrast to the drab backdrop of my daily life. I was instantly captivated by the sight of these mummers and *commedia dell'arte* players, their laughter and mirth a balm for my weary soul. And so, at the tender age of ten, I bade farewell to my fellow street urchins and joined their merry band, a bold and daring decision that would alter the course of my life forever.

My days as a guttersnipe, while filled with hardships and trials, served as the crucible in which my character was forged. The experiences of those early years shaped me into a resourceful, resilient individual, capable of adapting to any situation with ease and aplomb. Little did I know that this humble beginning would lay the foundation for a future filled with adventure, intrigue, and the pursuit of justice, as I would one day find myself at the very heart of the most baffling mysteries that the great city of London had ever known.

As I stepped into the vibrant world of street performance, I found myself utterly entranced by the dazzling array of characters that graced the makeshift stage. Each day was a whirlwind of rehearsals and performances, a never-ending parade of colour, sound, and emotion. At the heart of it all, I discovered a newfound sense of purpose and belonging, a feeling that had eluded me for the entirety of my short, tumultuous life.

Under the tutelage of the troupe's seasoned veterans, I quickly honed my skills as a performer, my innate talent for mimicry and deception proving invaluable in my pursuit of theatrical excellence. As the years passed, I became adept at slipping into the personas of a vast array of characters, my face a mutable canvas upon which I could paint any emotion or expression with consummate ease. This mastery of the actor's craft did not go unnoticed, and soon I was garnering accolades for my uncanny ability to bring even the most complex of roles to life. Working predominantly with half-masks, I also developed an expertise in interpreting body language and lip-reading, able to follow cues from my fellow actors with perfect timing and precision.

But it was in the realm of costume and disguise that I truly excelled, my nimble fingers fashioning the most intricate of ensembles from the simplest of materials. I found a particular delight in crafting wigs and masks, the transformative power of these adornments a constant source of wonder and fascination. In time, I became a chameleon, my ever-changing visage earning me the reputation of a master of disguise within the theatrical community.

As the troupe traversed the length and breadth of the British Isles, I continued my education; my insatiable curiosity driving me to study the art of makeup and prosthetics in my spare time. I became adept at altering my appearance on a whim, my skilful manipulations of colour and texture rendering me all but unrecognisable to even the most discerning of observers. It was not long before I was called upon to lend my talents to other productions, my expertise in the art of disguise earning me the moniker of the "Invisible Man" amongst my peers.

It was while securing the various venues for our performances that my familiarity with the criminal underclass was borne. After just a handful of 'mishaps' and dustups, the need to grease the palms of the crime lords and their minions became ever apparent. It was during those meetings in dark, noisy public houses that I developed an appreciation and respect of a sub-culture responsible for the inner workings of society that powered our so-called enlightened age. To secure the necessary protection and permissions, a network of agents expanded in every city.

But it was not all work and no play for this budding thespian, as my time with the troupe was also marked by a series of amorous dalliances and fleeting romances. Though none of these liaisons proved lasting, they served to further my education in the complex tapestry of human emotion, providing invaluable insight into the minds and hearts of those I encountered both on and off the stage.

In addition to my theatrical exploits, I also found myself drawn into the shadowy world of espionage, my unparalleled skills in disguise and subterfuge proving invaluable to those who sought to protect the interests of the British Empire. Though I was but a humble actor, I soon discovered that the line between fact and fiction was often blurred, as I found myself embroiled in a series of thrilling escapades that would have made even the most seasoned of secret agents green with envy.

By the time I reached the age of twenty-five, I had established myself as a force to be reckoned with in the world of theatre and espionage alike. My mastery of the arts of deception and disguise had brought me fame, fortune, and a measure of respect that I had never before thought possible, my once-humble origins all but a distant memory.

Yet, for all the success that had come my way, I remained restless, my soul yearning for new challenges and experiences that would test the limits of my considerable abilities. Little did I know that a later chapter of my life would bring me face to face with the most renowned detective the world had ever known, as well as the darkest and most insidious threats that the British Empire had ever faced. As fate would have it, my journey was only just beginning.

Having attained a considerable degree of proficiency in the thespian arts, I found myself ineluctably drawn towards the pursuit of further edification and greater challenges. I, therefore, set my sights on expanding my horizons and assuming the mantle of impresario, establishing a troupe that would rival even the most illustrious theatrical ensembles of the era. Thus, I embarked upon a new chapter in my life, brimming with ambition and an unquenchable thirst for artistic achievement.

During this period of my life, I found great pleasure in the cultivation of an extensive repertory of plays, ranging from the classical masterpieces of Shakespeare and Molière to the avant-garde works of emerging playwrights. This eclectic selection of productions served not only to showcase my own prodigious talents but also to provide a platform for the myriad talents of my fellow thespians, who had become an ersatz family to me over the years.

As the reputation of my troupe grew, so too did our opportunities for international travel. We found ourselves traversing the European continent, our performances met with great acclaim in the grandest of opera houses and the most intimate of playhouses alike. It was during these travels that I further honed my skills as a master of costume and disguise, my predilection for sartorial splendour and my proclivity for metamorphosis proving invaluable in our pursuit of theatrical perfection.

Indeed, my proficiency in the art of disguise extended beyond the stage, as I continued to engage in clandestine activities on behalf of the British Empire, from the Transvaal to Iskenderun. These covert operations necessitated the employment of a veritable panoply of aliases and personae, each meticulously crafted to facilitate the successful execution of my missions. My consummate skill in the art of deception proved instrumental in the circumvention of numerous intrigues and conspiracies that threatened the security and stability of the realm.

In addition to my exploits in the realm of espionage, I found great satisfaction in the expansion of my intellectual horizons. The pursuit of knowledge became an insatiable appetite, as I immersed myself in the study of languages, history, and the sciences, my indefatigable curiosity driving me to acquire a cornucopia of erudition. This scholarly inclination would later prove invaluable in my dealings with the enigmatic detective who would come to occupy the lodgings adjacent to my own.

By the time I reached the age of thirty, I had become a titan of the theatrical world, my accomplishments and accolades too numerous to enumerate. My troupe was renowned for our innovative productions and our unparalleled mastery of the dramatic arts, our reputation cemented as one of the foremost companies of the era. I had amassed a treasure trove of experiences and memories, each adventure more thrilling and enlightening than the last.

Yet, for all my successes and triumphs, a sense of ennui began to permeate my existence. The thrill of the stage, once so exhilarating and intoxicating, had begun to wane, the allure of fame and fortune no longer sufficient to quell the restless spirit that dwelled within me. I longed for a new challenge, a new purpose that would rekindle the fires of passion and ambition that had driven me throughout my life.

As I entered the fourth decade of my life, I found myself ensconced within the upper echelons of London's theatrical milieu, my reputation as a master of character acting and disguise having reached its zenith. The glittering pantheon of the West End had become my playground, my tireless dedication to the dramatic arts now firmly entrenched within the annals of theatrical history. I had reached the pinnacle of my profession, my name synonymous with excellence and innovation.

During this period, I turned my attentions towards the cultivation of new talent, my eye for prodigious skill and potential unerring in its discernment. I took great pleasure in guiding the careers of the fledgling actors and actresses who came under my tutelage, their meteoric rise to stardom a testament to my own prowess as a mentor and impresario. It was a source of immense pride to see the fruits of my labour flourish and prosper, the legacy of my own achievements living on through the accomplishments of those who followed in my footsteps.

My continued involvement in the shadowy realm of espionage further expanded my repertoire of skills, as I became a virtuoso of subterfuge and deception. My ability to infiltrate the most impenetrable of enemy strongholds, gather invaluable intelligence, and extricate myself from the most precarious of situations had become the stuff of legend within the clandestine circles in which I moved. My mastery of disguise and my preternatural talent for mimicry proved to be indispensable assets, my success in these covert endeavours further cementing my reputation as a man of many faces and talents.

Despite my prodigious achievements and the myriad accolades bestowed upon me, I remained a solitary figure, my heart untouched by the bonds of matrimony or the joys of parenthood. My personal life, much like my professional one, was characterised by a series of fleeting connections and transient dalliances, the mercurial nature of my existence precluding the formation of any lasting attachments. Yet, in my moments of introspection, I could not help but feel a pang of longing for the companionship and stability that had eluded me throughout my life.

As the years passed, I became increasingly aware of the inexorable march of time, the once-unquenchable fires of ambition and passion that had fuelled my meteoric rise now tempered by the wisdom and maturity that age had bestowed upon me. I began to contemplate the notion of retirement, my thoughts turning towards the pursuit of a quieter and more contemplative existence, one that would allow me to reflect upon the myriad adventures and experiences that had shaped my life.

It was at this juncture that a most unexpected turn of events would alter the course of my destiny, a fortuitous bequest that would irrevocably change the trajectory of my life. Sir Ignatius Brown, a gentleman of considerable wealth and influence, whom I had had the pleasure of encountering on several occasions during my theatrical career, passed away, leaving me a substantial portion of his vast fortune in his last will and testament.

This serendipitous windfall provided me with the means to retire from the world of theatre and espionage, affording me the opportunity to embrace a life of leisure, anonymity and contemplation. As I approached the age of fifty, I bid farewell to the glittering stages and shadowy intrigues that had been my home for so many years, my heart filled with a mixture of nostalgia and anticipation for the new chapter that lay before me.

And so, it was that I found myself in search of a suitable residence, a sanctuary where I could reflect upon the past and embrace the tranquillity and anonymity of the present. It was during this quest that I stumbled upon the quaint and unassuming environs of Baker Street, a locale that seemed to offer the perfect balance of seclusion and proximity to the bustling heart of London It was there that I secured lodgings at the venerable address of 221A, my new abode nestled adjacent to the dwelling of the most illustrious detective of the age, Mr Sherlock Holmes.

Chapter 1: Arrival in Baker Street

On a mild and sunny afternoon in the spring of 1889, I took leave of the hansom cab that had conveyed me from the train station to my new residence in Baker Street. As the spirited driver hastened away, I stood momentarily in front of the modest dwelling that was to be my home. I glanced at the neighbouring house and felt a thrill of excitement at the prospect of living next to the illustrious detective, Sherlock Holmes, a man whose extensive exploits I had passionately read on the very day of each publication.

"Mr Ollerenthorpe, I presume?" said a hearty voice from behind me. I turned to face an affable middle-aged gentleman, who carried himself with a certain air of importance.

"Indeed, sir," I replied, extending my hand. "And to whom do I have the pleasure of speaking?"

"Ah, forgive my manners," the man said, grasping my hand with a firm grip. "I am Mr Thaddeus Willoughby, your landlord. Welcome to Baker Street!"

"Thank you, Mr Willoughby," I replied. "I trust the house is in order?"

"Indeed, it is," he confirmed. "I have had it thoroughly cleaned and prepared for your arrival. I hope you shall find it satisfactory."

With that, Mr Willoughby handed me the keys, and we ascended the steps to the front door. Upon entering, I found the house to be neat and comfortably furnished. Mr Willoughby led me on a brief tour of the premises, during which he informed me that my new home had once belonged to an esteemed professor of botany who had recently passed away.

"I have taken the liberty of retaining much of the late professor's books, old newspapers and periodicals," Mr Willoughby informed me as we perused the well-stocked library. "I thought they might be of interest to you, being a learned man yourself."

"You are most thoughtful, Mr Willoughby," I replied, genuinely touched by his consideration. "I shall look forward to acquainting myself with the professor's collection."

Following the conclusion of our tour, Mr Willoughby took his leave, and I set about the task of unpacking my belongings. As I unpacked my possessions, my thoughts drifted to my new neighbour, the legendary Sherlock Holmes. I had long been an admirer of his exploits, as reported by his faithful friend and Boswell, Dr John Watson. I marvelled at the notion that the great detective himself lived but a stone's throw away and wondered if I might have the good fortune to make his acquaintance.

Several days passed as I gradually settled into my new surroundings. I found the house to be well-appointed and comfortable, and I spent many pleasant hours perusing the late professor's extensive library and collection of newspapers that went back many years. It was during one such evening, as I sat ensconced in a leather armchair with a treatise on entomology, that I heard the distinctive sound of a violin emanating from the neighbouring house.

I rose from my chair and approached the window, drawing the curtains aside ever so slightly. There, through the partially opened window of the adjacent house, I heard the unmistakable melodia of Sherlock Holmes, his unique phrasing of acoustics and hauntingly beautiful melody. The sound filled me with an ineffable sense of satisfaction; to think that I, Horatio Ollerenthorpe, was living next door to the world's most celebrated detective.

The following day, I decided to take a stroll around the neighbourhood, hoping that I might encounter Mr Holmes and make his acquaintance. As luck would have it, I had barely ventured more than a few steps from my front door when I quite literally stumbled into a gentleman of stout build and kind, if somewhat weary, countenance.

"Apologies, sir," I exclaimed, steadying myself. "I fear I was lost in thought and did not notice your approach."

"No harm done, sir," the gentleman responded with a warm smile. "I was similarly preoccupied, I must admit."

As I studied the man's whiskered features, I recognised him as none other than Dr John Watson, the trusted friend and confidant of Sherlock Holmes. My heart quickened at the prospect of meeting the great detective through such a fortuitous encounter.

"I am Horatio Ollerenthorpe, your new neighbour," I introduced myself, extending my hand. "Might you be Dr Watson?"

"Indeed, I am," he replied with jolly countenance, shaking my hand firmly. "It is a pleasure to make your acquaintance, Mr Ollerenthorpe. I trust you are finding Baker Street to your liking?"

"Very much so, Dr Watson," I confirmed. "And I must confess, I am most eager to meet your esteemed friend and colleague, Mr Holmes."

"Ah, well, you are in luck, Mr Ollerenthorpe," Watson said with a chuckle. "I am just on my way to see him now. Would you care to join me?"

"I would be most honoured, Dr Watson," I replied, scarcely able to contain my excitement.

Together, we crossed the short distance to the neighbouring house, and Dr Watson led me up the stairs to the sitting room that he and Holmes shared. Upon entering, I beheld Sherlock Holmes in person for the first time. He was reclining in a plush armchair, his long legs stretched out before him, and his sharp, hawk-like features partially obscured by a haze of thick, pungent pipe smoke. Billy, Holmes' page, stood diligently silent in the corner of the room.

"Holmes," Watson announced as he tucked into a box of sweetmeats, "I should like you to meet our new neighbour, Mr Horatio Ollerenthorpe."

Holmes regarded me with a cool, appraising gaze before rising to his feet and extending his hand. "Mr Ollerenthorpe," he said in a crisp, clear voice, "welcome to Baker Street."

"Thank you, Mr Holmes," I replied, feeling a thrill of excitement as I shook his hand. "I have long admired your work and am honoured to make your acquaintance."

Holmes offered a slight nod of acknowledgment but said little more, his countenance betraying an air of indifference that I found rather disheartening. I could not help but feel somewhat deflated by his cool demeanour, having anticipated a more engaging interaction with the renowned detective. As we engaged in polite conversation, I began to perceive that Holmes' manner was somewhat aloof and that his intellect, though undoubtedly formidable, did not seem as sharp as I had imagined from reading about his adventures in The Strand. He appeared preoccupied and disinterested, frequently casting his gaze towards the window as if yearning for a tantalising case to materialise before him, one that might sufficiently captivate his prodigious mind.

Dr Watson, ever the perceptive observer, sensed my disappointment and endeavoured to entice Holmes into the conversation with little success. "Holmes," he interjected, "I am certain that our esteemed guest would appreciate hearing your thoughts on the latest advancements in forensic science."

However, Holmes' response was lacklustre and insipid, a mere shadow of the brilliance I had come to expect from the great detective. Being a well-read individual, with an extensive library of non-fiction, it became disappointingly evident to me that his grasp on the subject was, in truth, rather tenuous, and his remarks were riddled with inaccuracies and oversights that one would scarcely expect from a man of his purported calibre.

Undeterred, Watson valiantly endeavoured to steer the conversation towards another topic, one that might perhaps elicit a more animated response from his enigmatic companion. "Perhaps, Holmes," he suggested, "you might regale our distinguished visitor with an account of our recent exploits in the case of the heist in Highgate, only published in The Times last week?" This was a story I had some familiarity with, as I was loosely acquainted with the criminal enterprise behind the larceny. Alas, Holmes' recollection of the events was woefully distorted, his narrative replete with errors and inconsistencies that could not have failed to strike even the most casual observer as indicative of a certain intellectual obtuseness. Indeed, it was as though he had been entirely disengaged from the proceedings, his mind occupied by some other, more pressing concern. I could not but feel a pang of disillusionment as I listened to his disjointed and muddled account, so far removed from the astute deductions and penetrating insights for which he was so renowned in print.

Watson, recognising the futility of his attempts to engage Holmes, adopted a more conciliatory approach. "Come now, Holmes," he said gently, "our guest is surely interested in more than just the minutiae of our professional life. Perhaps you could share some of your thoughts on the state of the world, or the future of our great nation?" And yet, even here, the great detective proved himself to be woefully ill-informed, his observations trite and insubstantial, lacking the depth and nuance one might reasonably expect from a man of his stature.

My previous excitement and anticipation, so keenly felt upon entering the sitting room at 221B Baker Street, had rapidly dissipated as I came to the disheartening realisation that the celebrated Sherlock Holmes was, in fact, likely a man of limited intellect and insight, his reputation seemingly founded upon the most tenuous of foundations. The great detective, it appeared, was but a pale shadow of the brilliant figure I had imagined him to be, a man far more adept at constructing an aura of infallibility than at delivering the prodigious feats of deduction for which he was so widely acclaimed.

As the conversation continued to meander ineffectually, I found myself reflecting upon the many tales of Holmes' extraordinary exploits that had captured my imagination, wondering how it could be that such a man, so seemingly devoid of the intellectual acuity that had once so captivated me, could have achieved such remarkable feats. Could it be, I pondered, that his success was attributable to some other, as yet unidentified factor, some hidden force that enabled him to transcend his apparent limitations and attain the heights of greatness to which he had so conspicuously ascended? Or, could it be simply explained by the post-rationalised imaginations of Dr John Watson?

It was not long before I took my leave, my initial excitement thoroughly dampened by the great detective's indifference and his apparent inability to engage meaningfully with the world around him. As I departed the hallowed chambers of 221B Baker Street, I could not help but feel a profound sense of disappointment, a melancholy realisation that the man I had once so admired was, in truth, little more than a hollow façade, a carefully constructed illusion that concealed a far more mundane reality.

Yet, even in the face of such disillusionment, a small part of me clung stubbornly to the belief that there must be more to Sherlock Holmes than met the eye, that beneath the surface of his disinterested exterior lay a wellspring of untapped potential, waiting for the right opportunity to reveal itself.

I resolved to learn more about the detective and, perhaps, to play some small part in his investigations. Little did I know that my curiosity would soon lead me down a path of intrigue and adventure that would forever change my life.

Chapter 2: The Disappointing Detective

Several weeks had passed since my first meeting with Sherlock Holmes. Although our initial encounter had left me somewhat disenchanted, I could not quell my curiosity about the man who had so captured the public's imagination. I resolved to observe him more closely in the hopes of understanding the secret to his success.

One morning, as I was reading the daily newspaper, I happened upon an article detailing a recent jewel theft. The thief had left a number of clues at the scene, including a blood-stained handkerchief, a broken watch chain, and a cryptic message hurriedly scrawled upon the wall. I could not help but wonder how Sherlock Holmes would approach such a case, and I eagerly awaited news of his involvement.

That very afternoon, as I was taking tea in my sitting room, I heard the sound of raised voices emanating from next door. I approached the window and, through the open casement, heard Sherlock Holmes and Dr Watson engaged in a heated discussion.

"Holmes, this is preposterous!" Dr Watson exclaimed in exasperation. "The thief left behind a veritable trail of breadcrumbs, and yet you insist on focusing on the irrelevant details!"

"Nonsense, Watson!" Holmes retorted; his voice tinged with indignation. "You fail to comprehend the subtleties of the case. The blood-stained handkerchief, for example, is a mere red herring designed to divert our attention from the true clues."

"But, Holmes," Watson protested, "the handkerchief bears the monogram of the victim, and the blood has been identified as belonging to the thief! Surely, this is a significant piece of evidence!"

"You are a man of science, Watson," Holmes replied dismissively, "and yet you allow yourself to be swayed by such superficialities. The broken watch chain and the cryptic message, on the other hand, are the keys to unlocking this mystery."

I listened in disbelief as Holmes proceeded to expound upon his convoluted theories, which seemed to grow increasingly far-fetched and nonsensical. It became apparent that the great detective was, in fact, an imbecile, prone to dismissing obvious clues and drawing wildly improbable conclusions. I could not fathom how a man of such limited intellect had achieved such renown, furthering my suspicion that his faithful friend and biographer, Dr Watson, had perhaps embellished the truth in his accounts of their adventures.

As the days went by, I continued to monitor Holmes' progress on the case, noting with amusement his repeated blunders and missteps. One particularly memorable incident occurred when, out of morbid curiosity I followed Holmes with Watson in tow, he insisted on interrogating a local florist in connection with the theft, based solely on the fact that the cryptic message on the wall had included a reference to roses.

"Mr Holmes, I assure you," the bewildered florist stammered, "I know nothing of this theft, nor do I have any knowledge of the mysterious message you speak of!"

"Ah, but that is precisely what a guilty man would say!" Holmes declared triumphantly. "You are clearly attempting to conceal your involvement in this nefarious crime!"

"But, Holmes," Dr Watson interjected, his patience clearly wearing thin, "the message refers to the Wars of the Roses, not to any actual flowers! It is a historical reference, not a clue pointing to a florist!"

Undeterred, Holmes continued his misguided line of questioning, much to the chagrin of both the florist and Dr Watson. I could not help but feel a certain degree of sympathy for the beleaguered doctor, who seemed to bear the brunt of his partner's ineptitude.

The final straw came when Holmes, in a fit of misplaced enthusiasm, decided to stake out the residence of a noted historian, convinced that the man held the key to deciphering the cryptic message. Armed with a pair of opera glasses and a false moustache, Holmes positioned himself in an alleyway across the street from the historian's home, prepared for a night of furtive observation.

Dr Watson, who had reluctantly agreed to accompany Holmes on his ill-conceived surveillance mission, soon grew weary of the charade. As the hours dragged on and the historian failed to reveal any incriminating behaviour, Watson finally reached the limits of his patience.

"Holmes, this is patently absurd," Watson hissed in a hushed whisper. "We have wasted an entire evening watching a man read books and sip tea in his sitting room! And I have missed my dinner! The solution to the crime lies in the evidence we already have, not in the habits of an innocent historian!"

Holmes, however, remained steadfast in his conviction, insisting that the historian would eventually reveal his nefarious intentions. As the night wore on and dawn began to break, even Holmes was forced to concede that their vigil had been in vain. The trail of the villain had gone well and truly cold, and the jewels, no doubt, distributed amongst the nefarious network of fences spread across our metropolis.

I found myself consumed by a desire to rectify the situation. If Sherlock Holmes, the great detective, was truly nothing more than a bungling imbecile, then it fell to someone else to solve the crimes that plagued London's streets. I determined that I would be that someone, and that I would use my own considerable intellect and powers of observation to bring justice to those who sought it.

Thus, I embarked upon a secret campaign to aid Sherlock Holmes in his investigations, anonymously providing him with the clues and insights he so sorely lacked. I would be the invisible hand that guided the great detective, the unseen force that propelled him to greatness. And, perhaps, in doing so, I would find some measure of satisfaction in the knowledge that I had played a part in solving the mysteries that had long captivated my imagination.

As I sat in my study, I could not help but feel a sense of excitement at the prospect of what lay ahead. Little did I know that my clandestine efforts would lead me down a path of intrigue and danger, forging an unspoken bond between myself and the bumbling detective who lived next door.

And so, with a steely determination and a newfound sense of purpose, I set to work, carefully crafting a series of anonymous telegrams that would provide Sherlock Holmes with the guidance he so desperately needed. In doing so, I began a new chapter in my life, one that would forever intertwine my fate with that of the most celebrated detective in all of London.

In the ensuing days, I found myself engrossed in the peculiar task I had undertaken, secretly witnessing Sherlock Holmes in his investigations from the open window of my own sitting room. From this modest perch, I would spend countless hours listening to Holmes and Watson as they discussed their latest cases, oblivious to my presence. I found their conversations to be a source of both amusement and frustration, as I marvelled at the absurdity of Holmes' deductions and the patient forbearance of his long-suffering companion.

One evening, as I stood at my window with a glass of claret in hand, I overheard a particularly frustrating exchange between the two. They were discussing a peculiar case I had read about in the newspaper that very afternoon, where a priceless painting had been stolen and replaced with a convincing forgery that bore the unmistakable touch of an experienced craftsman's expert hand.

"Clearly, Watson," Holmes declared with great conviction, "the culprit is none other than the victim's own twelve-year-old nephew! The boy's fondness for painting, coupled with his access to the residence, make him the prime suspect in this dastardly crime!"

"But, Holmes," Watson protested, his voice tinged with disbelief, "surely you cannot be serious! The child is but a mere innocent, and the notion that he could have orchestrated such a complex heist is patently absurd!"

"Ah, but that is where you are mistaken, my dear Watson," Holmes replied smugly, his voice elevated with the thrill of his own imagined cleverness. "The boy's youthful innocence is but a clever ruse, a cunning façade designed to mask his true nature as a criminal mastermind!"

I listened in silent incredulity as Holmes spun a fantastical tale of intrigue and deception, implicating the hapless child in a far-reaching conspiracy that extended to the highest echelons of the art world. It was a preposterous theory, one that ignored the more plausible explanation that the theft had been the work of an experienced criminal with connections to the art underworld.

Determined to set the ridiculous detective off his current path, and to abandon his misguided pursuit of the innocent child. I penned an anonymous telegram, providing him with several key pieces of information that I had managed to glean from my own observations and experience. I urged him to focus his attention on the high probability that the perpetrator is an art forger. To that end, the note contained the name and location of a notorious dealer in counterfeit art, known to be active in London, with tentacles of influence that span the entire cohort of forgers within the region, most probably including our elusive quarry.

The following day, as I once again took up my position at the window, I was gratified to hear that Holmes had, at least to some extent, heeded my advice. Although he continued to harbour suspicions about the young boy, he had grudgingly conceded that an art forger was a more likely lead and had set about investigating his possible involvement in the crime.

However, true to form, Holmes' attempts to apprehend the forger proved to be a comedy of errors. He contrived to disguise himself as a fine art collector in the hopes of luring the counterfeit art dealer into a trap, only to find himself ensnared in a web of his own making. His elaborate ruse was undone by his own ineptitude, as he unwittingly revealed his true identity to the forger, whilst attempting to purchase a counterfeit painting.

"Mr Holmes," the dealer sneered, as he exposed the detective's poorly executed disguise, "your reputation as a master of disguise is, I fear, somewhat exaggerated. You would do well to leave the art of deception to those who are better suited to its practice."

Undeterred, I began by conducting a thorough examination of the forged painting, which had been recovered by the police following Holmes' botched attempt to apprehend the dealer. As I scrutinised the canvas, I noticed a peculiar detail that had eluded both Holmes and the authorities – a small, almost imperceptible, mark hidden within the brushstrokes of the forgery.

With the assistance of an old acquaintance, a senior curator in the National Portrait Gallery, I soon discovered that this mark was an important clue. The mark was a unique signature employed by a highly skilled forger who had long eluded the grasp of the London police. Known only as "The Chameleon," this mysterious figure had developed a reputation for his uncanny ability to replicate the works of the great masters, leaving behind only the subtlest of clues to betray the true nature of his creations.

With this important knowledge, I set about tracing the origins of the forged painting, following a trail of clues that led me deep into the seedy underbelly of the London art world. Along the way, I encountered a cast of colourful characters, including a plethora of unscrupulous art dealers, cunning thieves, and even a reclusive painter who claimed to have once been the protégé of the elusive Chameleon.

As I delved deeper into the mystery, I continued to provide Holmes with anonymous telegrams, gently nudging him in the right direction whilst taking care to maintain my own invisibility. Despite my best efforts, however, the great detective seemed to possess an uncanny knack for misinterpreting my carefully crafted clues, leading him to embark upon a series of wild goose chases that served only to further muddy the waters.

In one particularly memorable incident, Holmes became convinced that the mark I had discovered was, in fact, the insignia of a secret society of Freemasons, leading him to infiltrate a covert meeting in the hopes of unmasking the forger. Disguised as a lowly initiate, he managed to gain entry to the gathering, only to be unmasked midway through the proceedings when his ill-fitting wig fell off, revealing himself to the assembled brethren.

Undeterred by this latest humiliation, Holmes continued to pursue the forger with dogged determination, blundering his way through a series of improbable adventures that seemed to owe more to the pages of a penny dreadful than the annals of a great detective. And yet, through it all, I remained steadfast in my resolve to guide him towards the truth, even as I despaired of his ever achieving the greatness to which he so clearly aspired.

It was after many a sleepless night, and countless hours poring over my intricate network of informants and resources, that the veil of mystery surrounding the enigmatic Chameleon finally began to lift. What emerged from the tangled web of deceit and misdirection was a portrait of a man driven to the brink of despair by the cruel machinations of fate, a man who had once shone brightly in the firmament of the art world but had now become lost in the shadows of criminality.

In my unrelenting pursuit of the truth, I had scoured the annals of artistic history, delving into the murky depths of forgotten scandals and long-buried secrets. It was during these exhaustive inquiries that I chanced upon the tragic tale of Percival Hargreaves, a man whose extraordinary talents had once earned him the adulation of critics and collectors alike, but whose star had fallen from grace in a maelstrom of disgrace and recrimination.

As I perused the tattered newspaper clippings and yellowed correspondence that chronicled the rise and fall of this erstwhile prodigy, I could not help but feel a twinge of sympathy for the man whose life had been so cruelly derailed by the vicissitudes of fortune. The fateful liaison that had precipitated his downfall had been, by all accounts, a tempestuous affair, a whirlwind romance that had left in its wake a trail of broken hearts and shattered dreams. And it was in the smouldering embers of this ill-fated tryst that the seeds of vengeance had been sown, a bitter harvest that would ultimately yield the poisoned fruit of the Chameleon's nefarious enterprise.

Having unmasked the man behind the Chameleon's many guises, I set about piecing together the intricate mosaic of his criminal activities, a painstaking endeavour that required the utmost diligence and discretion. Through a series of clandestine meetings and surreptitious exchanges, I gradually uncovered the full extent of his perfidious scheme, a labyrinthine plot that had ensnared the very upper echelons of the art world in a web of forgery and deception.

In my quest for justice, I knew that I must tread carefully, for the Chameleon was a cunning adversary whose chimerical nature made him a most elusive quarry. Armed with the incontrovertible evidence of his crimes, I prepared to confront the man, by proxy, who had once been Percival Hargreaves, a man whose genius had been twisted by the bitter sting of betrayal and whose heart had been consumed by the insatiable fires of revenge.

And so, with the ineluctable passage of time, the final act of this sordid drama was set to unfold, a denouement that would see the Chameleon unmasked and the dark secrets of his past laid bare for all the world to see.

I promptly dispatched a telegram to Holmes, providing him with the information he needed to apprehend the forger and bring him to justice. Upon receipt of my missive, Holmes and Watson hastily prepared themselves for the conclusion of this most peculiar and convoluted case. Ensconced in my familiar vantage point by the window, I observed the duo as they emerged from the safety of their lodgings, clad in an assortment of outlandish garments and accoutrements that they deemed essential to their preposterous plan. Fearing a calamitous end, I despatched a street Arab, sharp as a tack and recently under my employ, to observe the duo from the shadows and to report back how events were to unfold. Plus, the urchin was instructed to call in an Inspector Lestrade, an acquaintance of Holmes, and the constabulary if the situation were to deviate down a dangerous path.

As they set forth on their quixotic quest to apprehend the elusive Chameleon, I could not help but feel a pang of trepidation at the prospect of these two hapless sleuths attempting to navigate the labyrinthine intricacies of the criminal underworld. And yet, in spite of their myriad shortcomings and idiosyncrasies, there was something undeniably endearing about their dogged determination and unswerving belief in their own abilities.

In their pursuit, Holmes and Watson employed a smorgasbord of disguises and subterfuges, each more outlandish and farcical than the last. One moment they would adopt the guise of roving street performers, regaling passers-by with their preposterous feats of juggling and prestidigitation; the next, they would transform themselves into ragged beggars or disreputable ne'er-do-wells, lurking in the shadows of London's seedier quarters in the hope of ensnaring their quarry.

During the course of their investigations, the pair conducted a series of increasingly elaborate and far-fetched ruses in their efforts to penetrate the Chameleon's inner sanctum, a campaign of subterfuge that frequently bordered on the absurd. There were veiled rendezvous in dimly lit taverns, surreptitious exchanges of secret codes and handshakes, and even an audacious attempt to infiltrate the Chameleon's lair through an improbably narrow chimney.

At last, after a series of misadventures and near misses that would have been comical if not for the gravity of their mission, the intrepid duo found themselves face to face with their quarry. In a scene that could have been lifted from the script of a back-street comedy, Holmes and Watson confronted the Chameleon in his subterranean workshop, the walls of which were adorned with the counterfeit masterpieces that bore testament to his prodigious talents and malevolent ambition.

As the two detectives launched into a verbose and histrionic denunciation of the forger's crimes, the Chameleon listened with an air of bemused detachment, his eyes twinkling with a mixture of amusement and contempt. It was clear that he regarded his pursuers as little more than an annoyance, a pair of bumbling amateurs who had blundered their way into his domain through sheer dumb luck and blind persistence.

Having the tale recounted later that evening by my hidden spy, I could not help but marvel at the extraordinary nexus of circumstances that had led to this denouement. The confluence of serendipity and fortuity had conspired to render the Chameleon's capture almost farcical in its absurdity.

Holmes, in an utterly misguided attempt to apprehend the miscreant, had accidentally stumbled upon an exiguous tripwire, causing a cascade of precariously balanced *objets d'art* to drop a large portrait of 'some posh geezer' onto the head of the hapless villain, his astonished face poking through the centre of the canvas, momentarily rendering him insensate. Watson, ever the stalwart companion, had executed an ungainly and ill-considered leap to avoid the cascading debris, inadvertently landing atop the Chameleon and effectively pinning him to the ground. His game was well and truly up.

"What an extraordinary concatenation of events, Holmes!" Watson panted, his countenance a mixture of astonishment and relief. "It seems that the fickle finger of fate has conspired in our favour this time."

"Indeed, my dear Watson," Holmes replied, a touch of pomposity evident in his voice. "It would appear that our quarry has been hoisted with his own petard, as it were. A fitting end for one who has so consistently eluded the grasp of justice."

With the unceremonious clatter of shackles and the solemn intonation of the constabulary's charge, the Chameleon's criminal career was brought to an ignominious end. As the tale culminated in him being led away to face the consequences of his misdeeds, I could not help but feel a certain sense of satisfaction in the knowledge that my clandestine intervention had played a pivotal role in the resolution of this most extraordinary case.

With my guidance, the great detective had managed to apprehend the notorious Chameleon, restoring the stolen painting to its rightful owner, and securing a small measure of justice for the victims of the forger's nefarious schemes. As news of Holmes' triumph spread throughout the city, his reputation as a master sleuth was once again solidified, much to the bemusement of those who knew the true extent of his ineptitude.

For my part, I was content to remain in the shadows, an invisible force guiding the hand of fate. Though I knew that I would never receive the accolades and admiration that were heaped upon the great detective, I took solace in the knowledge that my own intellect and powers of observation had played a crucial role in solving the mystery of the stolen painting.

In the days that followed, I continued to watch Holmes and Watson from my window, observing their comings and goings with a mixture of amusement and bemusement. I knew that it was only a matter of time before they would be called upon to unravel another baffling crime, and I vowed to be ready to assist them in their efforts, as the unseen partner in their adventures.

As I sat in my study, sipping a glass of claret and reflecting on the events that had brought me to this strange juncture in my life, I could not help but feel a sense of anticipation for the future. For, in my new role as the silent guardian of Sherlock Holmes, I had found a purpose that I had long been seeking, a way to use my own considerable intellect to make a difference in the world.

And so, as the sun set on another day in the great city of London, I raised my glass in a silent toast to the bumbling detective who lived next door and the extraordinary partnership that had been forged in the shadows. Together, we would face the challenges that lay ahead, unravelling the mysteries of the human heart and bringing justice to those who sought it, all from the quiet sanctuary of my humble abode.

To the world, I was Horatio Ollerenthorpe, a mild-mannered gentleman of leisure with a passion for the written word. But, in the privacy of my own mind, I knew that I was something more – a silent partner in the great detective's exploits, an invisible hand guiding him towards the truth.

Chapter 3: The Savoy Bomb Plot

As the warm sun of August shone down upon the bustling streets of London, casting its golden glow upon the city's ancient edifices and its teeming throngs of humanity, I found myself once again ensconced in the sanctuary of my sitting room, a glass of *crème de menthe* in hand and a volume of poetry in my lap. Yet, as I attempted to lose myself in the evocative verses of Tennyson and the timeless beauty of his words, I found my thoughts continually drawn to the curious events that had unfolded in the preceding weeks.

I was roused from my reverie by the sound of barely hushed voices emanating from the sitting room of my illustrious neighbour, Sherlock Holmes. Straining to catch the words of their conversation, I discerned that Holmes had been visited by a gentleman who seemed to be in a state of considerable distress.

Intrigued by the prospect of yet another perplexing case, I set aside my book and approached the window, hoping to learn the identity of the mysterious visitor. To my surprise, I learned that the visitor was none other than Mr Gerald Goldenstein, the esteemed manager of the soon-to-be-opened Savoy Hotel, which had been the subject of much anticipation and intrigue in the London press.

As I turned my ear toward the window, I heard Holmes begin his customary *cold reading* of his potential client, before Mr Goldenstein could begin disclosing the source of his peril.

"Mr Goldenstein, I observe that you conveyed yourself on foot, by the hue of the dust on your shoes, and that you recently were blessed with offspring. I must congratulate you and Mrs Goldenstein on your new arrival."

Annoyed and perplexed, Mr Goldenstein retorted. "Actually, Mr Holmes, I arrived by a private carriage belonging to the hotel. And you are completely mistaken; I am a confirmed bachelor."

Holmes spluttered and was keen to move onto a different subject. "Pray, describe the reason for your visit."

As I continue to listen, I heard Mr Goldenstein relate a chilling tale of extortion and terror. It seemed that the hotel had been threatened by a shadowy figure who had demanded the princely sum of £1,000, warning that, should his demands not be met, a bomb would be detonated within the hotel's walls on the day of its grand opening. The note had been delivered to Mr Goldenstein with strict instructions not to involve the police, leaving him with little choice but to seek the aid of the so-called great detective.

Holmes, never one to shy away from a challenge, listened attentively to Mr Goldenstein's tale, his eyes likely narrowing in thought as he considered the implications of the case. "It is clear to me," he declared, after a moment's reflection, "that we are dealing with an Irish separatist sympathiser, intent on sowing chaos and destruction in the heart of our great city. The use of a bomb as a weapon of terror is a hallmark of these radical agitators, and the target – a symbol of opulence and decadence – is a natural choice for their flagitious aims."

I could not help but shake my head in disbelief at the great detective's hasty and, to my mind, wholly unfounded conclusion. While it was true that the use of explosives had become something of a calling card for certain radical elements, it seemed to me that there was little in the details of Mr Goldenstein's account to suggest that this plot was the work of such a group.

Undeterred by my silent scepticism, Holmes set about devising a plan to unmask the would-be bomber and avert the impending disaster. As he and Watson discussed various strategies, ranging from the plausible to the patently absurd, I decided that it was once again incumbent upon me to take matters into my own hands and seek out the truth behind the Savoy bomb plot.

Retreating to the sanctuary of my study, I began to pore over the pages of my extensive collection of newspapers, searching for any mention of similar incidents or patterns of criminal activity that might provide a clue to the identity of the perpetrator. After several hours of diligent research, I came across an account of a failed bomb plot at the Great Eastern Hotel in 1884, some five years previous, which bore striking similarities to the present case.

The culprit in that instance had been a criminal by the name of Wilfred Blackwood, a man with a history of extortion and a penchant for explosives. I was struck by the uncanny resemblance between the *modus operandi* of the Great Eastern Hotel plot and the one now threatening the Savoy. It seemed to me that I had stumbled upon a critical piece of the puzzle, one that had eluded the great detective in his haste to pin the blame on a convenient scapegoat.

Armed with this new information, I decided to pay a visit to Scotland Yard, hoping to gather further details on Blackwood's past and his escape from the clutches of the law. Disguising myself as a journalist, I managed to secure an interview with Inspector Lestrade, who had been involved in the original investigation into the Great Eastern Hotel plot.

As we discussed the case, I discovered that Blackwood had been a cunning and resourceful criminal, adept at covering his tracks and evading capture. In the previous year of 1888, he had escaped incarceration by way of a carefully orchestrated affair, involving a network of accomplices and an intimate knowledge of the prison's weaknesses.

The more I learned of Blackwood's exploits, the more convinced I became that he was the true mastermind behind the Savoy bomb plot. It seemed to me that he had returned to his old ways, seeking once again to terrorise the citizens of London and line his own pockets in the process.

As I thanked Inspector Lestrade for his time and took my leave of Scotland Yard, I resolved to provide Holmes with the information he needed to apprehend Blackwood and avert the impending disaster at the Savoy. Yet, as I prepared to dispatch my latest anonymous telegram, I could not help but feel a certain sense of trepidation.

Would the great detective be able to see through the fog of his own prejudices and recognise the truth that lay before him? Or would he continue to chase after phantom separatist conspiracies, blind to the real danger that threatened the city he had sworn to protect?

As I returned to my lodgings and watched the sun dip below the horizon, casting the streets of London in an eerie twilight, I could only hope that, with my guidance, Holmes would be able to unravel the twisted threads of the Savoy bomb plot and bring the true culprit to justice. For the lives of countless innocent people now hung in the balance, and time was running out for the city I called home.

With a growing sense of urgency, I set about crafting a plan to convey my findings to Sherlock Holmes in a manner that would not arouse suspicion. It occurred to me that a newspaper clipping, slipped discreetly through the letterbox of 221B Baker Street, might serve my purposes admirably. Selecting an article detailing Blackwood's criminal history and daring escape, I penned a note in the margin, drawing attention to the striking similarities between the Great Eastern Hotel plot and the current threat facing the Savoy.

Late that evening, under the cover of darkness, I ventured forth to deliver the missive, hoping against hope that it would be enough to persuade Holmes to reconsider his misguided theory. As I retreated to the safety of my own residence, I watched through the window as the hapless detective retrieved the clipping from his doorstep, his brow furrowed in concentration as he read the words I had so carefully inscribed.

To my dismay, however, it seemed that my efforts were in vain. For, rather than embracing the verisimilitude of the evidence before him, Holmes dismissed the notion that Blackwood could be involved, stubbornly clinging to his belief that a separatist sympathiser was the true culprit. As he cast the newspaper aside and returned to his previous line of inquiry, I felt a surge of frustration and disappointment.

Realising that it was now up to me to unmask Blackwood and thwart his nefarious plans, I decided to redouble my efforts and track down the elusive criminal myself. Using the information gleaned from my research and my conversation with Inspector Lestrade, I began to piece together the threads of Blackwood's life, searching for any clue that might lead me to his current whereabouts.

After several days of dogged investigation, I discovered that Blackwood hailed from the picturesque town of Taunton in Somerset. Recalling that criminals often returned to familiar haunts when in hiding, I consulted my trusty Bradshaw's Guide and made my way to Taunton by the next express from Paddington, hoping to find some trace of the man I now considered my quarry.

Upon arriving in the quaint town, I began making discreet inquiries about Blackwood, being cautious not to arouse suspicion or alert him to my presence. I resolved to conduct my initial inquiries within the confines of the local public house, a veritable nexus of information and gossip in such provincial settings. Donning the guise of an inebriated vagabond, I endeavoured to ingratiate myself with the patrons of the establishment, my dishevelled appearance and slurred speech serving to allay any suspicions that I was naught but a humble drunkard seeking solace in the amber embrace of alcohol.

It was not long before I found myself engaged in conversation with the publican, a furtive and somewhat oleaginous individual who appeared to harbour a wealth of knowledge regarding the local populace and their affairs. I deftly steered the discourse towards the subject of Mr Blackwood, my insistent queries and oblique insinuations gradually wearing down the landlord's initial reticence.

"My good sir," I began, the words issuing forth from my lips in a mellifluous drawl, "listen, listen. Once 'pon a time, 'twas a bloke... bloke called Blackwood. Yeah, Blackwood. He... he used to... used to hang 'round here, you know. I'd like... I'd like to, y'know, meet 'im. Some busy-ness to… discuss. Got any... any idea where this Blackwood fella might be these days? Eh?"

The landlord cast a furtive glance about the dimly lit tavern, his countenance betraying a hint of wariness as he considered my request. "I do believe I know of the gentleman to whom you refer," he replied hesitantly, his voice barely audible above the cacophony of laughter and clinking glasses that filled the room. "However, I fear I cannot assist you in locating him, as he has not been seen in these parts for quite some time."

Undeterred, I pressed on, my persistence eventually yielding the desired result. "Ey, ya might know any of his kin or pals who can gimme the goods I'm lookin' for, eh?" I inquired, my tone tinged with just the right amount of desperation and beseeching.

The landlord, sensing an opportunity to rid himself of my importunate presence, finally relented. "Very well," he acquiesced, his voice now little more than a conspiratorial whisper. "It is said that Blackwood's mother lives in a humble abode on the outskirts of the village, the precise location of which I can provide if you promise to quit your prying and bugger off!"

I readily assented to his terms, my heart swelling with triumph as the landlord divulged the coveted information. With the address of Blackwood's mother now firmly in my possession, I made a hasty exit from the tavern, my mind already racing ahead to the next stage of my investigation, the elusive figure of Blackwood inching ever closer to my grasp.

Eventually, I arrived at a small cottage on the outskirts of Taunton, where Blackwood's elderly mother still resided. While it seemed a long shot that the notorious criminal would seek refuge with a family member, I resolved to investigate the lead, as it was the only connection to Blackwood I had uncovered.

As I approached the modest dwelling, nestled amidst a grove of ancient oak trees, I felt my heart race with a mixture of excitement and trepidation. Could it be that I was on the verge of apprehending the mastermind behind the Savoy bomb plot, succeeding where the great Sherlock Holmes had so spectacularly failed?

Steeling myself for the confrontation that lay ahead, I cautiously made my way to the cottage door, my senses on high alert for any sign of danger. Little did I know that the events that were about to unfold would test the limits of my courage and cunning, and ultimately determine the fate of the Savoy Hotel and all those who dwelled within its hallowed halls.

With a deep breath, I rapped firmly on the cottage door, my ears straining to detect any sounds of movement from within. After a seemingly interminable wait, the door creaked open to reveal a frail, elderly woman with a wizened face and eyes that bore the weight of a lifetime of sorrows.

"Good afternoon, madam," I began, adopting the air of a traveling salesman. "I was wondering if I might have a moment of your time to discuss a most advantageous offer."

The woman hesitated for a moment, her gaze flicking nervously to the interior of the cottage before she replied in a wavering voice, "I'm afraid I'm not interested, sir. I have all I need, and my son provides for me when he can."

I seized upon her mention of her son, pressing gently, "Ah, your son. Would that be Mr Wilfred Blackwood, by any chance?"

A flicker of fear crossed the woman's face, and she attempted to close the door. "I don't know what you're talking about," she stammered. "My son has nothing to do with any trouble. Now, if you'll excuse me…"

But I was not to be deterred. "Please, madam," I implored, dropping the act and softening my voice. "I am not here to cause any harm. I merely wish to speak with your son to prevent a terrible tragedy from occurring."

The woman hesitated, her eyes filling with tears as she considered my words. At last, she stepped aside, granting me entry into the humble dwelling. "He's upstairs," she whispered, her voice barely audible. "But please, I beg you, do not hurt him."

I ascended the narrow staircase, my heart pounding in my chest as I contemplated the confrontation that awaited me. Upon reaching the top of the stairs, I found myself facing a door, slightly ajar, from which emanated the faint sounds of laboured breathing.

Summoning all my courage, I pushed the door open to reveal a small, dimly-lit room, its walls lined with shelves crammed with an assortment of chemicals and explosive materials. And there, hunched over a workbench, his face pale and gaunt, was the man I had been searching for: Wilfred Blackwood.

As Blackwood looked up from his work, his eyes widened in surprise and fear. "Who are you?" he demanded, his voice hoarse. "How did you find me?"

"Your past has caught up with you, Blackwood," I replied, my voice steady despite the pounding of my heart. "I know of your plot to bomb the Savoy Hotel, and I am here to put an end to it."

Blackwood sneered, a dangerous glint in his eye. "You think you can stop me?" he spat. "I've evaded the police for years, and I won't be thwarted by the likes of you."

As we stood there, locked in a tense standoff, I knew that I had but one chance to bring Blackwood to justice and avert the catastrophe that loomed over the Savoy. And as I prepared to make my move, I silently prayed that the skills I had honed on the stage would be enough to see me through the perilous encounter that lay ahead.

Aware that the element of surprise was my greatest asset, I lunged towards Blackwood, my goal being to subdue him before he could react. However, the seasoned criminal was quicker than I had anticipated, and he managed to evade my grasp, darting towards the window.

In the chaos of our struggle, I noticed a stick of explosive lying on the workbench. I seized the opportunity to snatch it as evidence, knowing that it would lend credence to my claims about Blackwood's involvement in the Savoy bomb plot. With the explosive in hand, I made a hasty retreat, racing down the stairs and out of the cottage before Blackwood could recover from his shock.

Once a safe distance from the cottage, I paused to catch my breath and consider my next move. Despite having found Blackwood, I was no closer to stopping his plan to bomb the Savoy Hotel. I knew that I would need Holmes's assistance to apprehend the cunning criminal and bring him to justice, yet I could not risk exposing my identity to the great detective.

As I pondered my predicament, an idea began to take shape in my mind. If I could provide Holmes with Blackwood's location, perhaps he would reconsider his previous assumptions and pursue the true culprit behind the bomb plot. And so, with renewed determination, I returned to London, the stick of explosive carefully concealed in my satchel.

Upon reaching Baker Street, I quickly penned a note detailing Blackwood's whereabouts and the explosive evidence I had discovered. Folding both the note around the stick of dynamite, I slipped it through the letterbox of 221B, hoping that this time, Holmes would heed my warning and act upon the information I had provided.

As I retreated to the safety of my own residence, I could only wait and pray that the puzzling detective would recognise the gravity of the situation and abandon his misguided theories in favour of the truth that lay before him. For, with each passing moment, the threat to the Savoy Hotel and the lives of its unsuspecting guests grew ever more imminent, and the fate of countless innocent souls hung in the balance.

As the hours ticked by, I watched anxiously from my window, my gaze fixed on the entrance to Holmes's lodgings. And then, just as I was beginning to fear that my efforts had once again been in vain, I saw the detective emerge from his residence, a determined look in his eye as he hailed a cab and set off in the direction of the train station.

With a sigh of relief, I allowed myself a small moment of satisfaction, knowing that I had done all I could to avert the disaster that threatened the Savoy Hotel. Now, the outcome of the case lay in the hands of Sherlock Holmes, and I could only hope that, with the guidance I had provided, the great detective would at last apprehend the cunning mastermind behind the bomb plot and restore peace to the streets of London.

Several days passed before I caught sight of Sherlock Holmes returning to Baker Street, his countenance one of self-congratulatory triumph. I could hardly contain my curiosity as I strained to catch snippets of conversation between Holmes and his faithful companion, Dr Watson, through my ever-convenient window.

"Ah, Watson," Holmes crowed, "I have at last apprehended the scoundrel behind the dastardly Savoy bomb plot! It was a stroke of sheer genius on my part, I must say."

Dr Watson, ever the loyal friend, nodded his agreement whilst tucking into his second strawberry tart. "Indeed, Holmes," said Watson whilst spluttering crumbs onto the carpet, "your deductions were most impressive. But tell me, how did you come to suspect that the culprit was hiding in Taunton?"

Holmes puffed out his chest, eager to regale his friend with the tale of his brilliance. "Well, you see, Watson, it all began when I received an anonymous note, wrapped around a stick of explosive, containing an address in Taunton. At first, I dismissed it as irrelevant, for I was convinced that our quarry was aboard a ship bound from Ireland."

I shook my head in bemusement, marvelling at Holmes's ability to misconstrue even the most obvious of clues and explicit instructions. The detective continued, oblivious to my silent derision.

"I hurried to the train station, intending to intercept the ship at Liverpool. But while aboard the first-class carriage, it suddenly dawned upon me that the address in Taunton could, in fact, be the very lair of our elusive criminal. I promptly disembarked and raced southward to the sleepy town, accompanied by the ever-competent Inspector Lestrade and his men."

"As we approached the cottage, we found it deserted, but a thorough search of the abandoned premises in the area soon revealed an outbuilding filled with explosives and damning evidence of Blackwood's guilt. Lestrade's men quickly apprehended the scoundrel as he attempted to flee the scene, and the villain has been safely ensconced in a prison cell ever since."

Watson listened with rapt attention, his admiration for his friend's deductive prowess undiminished by the farcical nature of Holmes's account. "Splendid work, Holmes," he enthused. "You have once again proven yourself to be the foremost detective of our time."

As I listened into the pair's self-congratulatory conversation, I felt a mixture of frustration and amusement at Holmes's continued idiocy. It seemed that, despite my best efforts, the great detective remained stubbornly blind to the truth of his own incompetence.

Yet, as the sun set over Baker Street, casting long shadows across the familiar cobblestones, I could not help but feel a certain satisfaction in my clandestine role as the guiding hand behind Sherlock Holmes's adventures. For, while he might never know the true extent of my involvement, I could take comfort in the knowledge that my efforts had averted disaster and brought a dangerous criminal to justice.

And so, as I retreated from my vantage point at the window, I resolved to continue my secret partnership with the unwitting Holmes, ever vigilant and ready to step in when his imbecility threatened to derail the course of justice. For in this world of shadows and deception, I, Horatio Ollerenthorpe, had become the unseen guardian of London's peace, the silent sentinel watching over the city from behind the veil of anonymity.

Chapter 4: The Horse Owners' Peril

One fateful morning, as I sat by my window enjoying a steaming cup of Darjeeling tea, my attention was drawn to a carriage pulling up before 221B Baker Street. A tall, elegant woman alighted from the vehicle, her eyes darting nervously about as she approached the door of Sherlock Holmes's residence. I could not help but feel a spark of curiosity at the sight of this new potential client, and I settled in to observe the unfolding drama.

After being admitted into Holmes's lodgings by the page Billy, the woman introduced herself as Mrs. Constance Worthington, and, without being asked, wasted no time in revealing the cause of her distress. She had discovered a most alarming scene in her stables: her favourite mare, once spritely and *et-epimeletic*, showed an unprecedented apprehension and unwillingness to be ridden. Mrs Worthington had also discovered sugar-cubes strewn about the ground; a foodstuff banned from the stables on account of its detriment to dental hygiene. Moreover, the equine's gender had changed, overnight. Despite her initial panic, Mrs. Worthington had had the presence of mind to seek the assistance of the great detective in solving this bizarre mystery.

As Holmes listened to her tale, his countenance took on the semblance of a master in action. "Most intriguing, madam," he declared, rising from his armchair with a flourish. "A case worthy of my unique talents, to be sure. Before you continue, allow me to deduce some facts about you and your mode of travel to my humble abode."

Mrs. Worthington looked on in amazement as Holmes began to circle her, scrutinising every detail of her appearance. After several moments of what sounded like intense, silent observation, the detective announced, "The faint aroma of the city clings to your garments, suggesting that your home lies in an urban setting. It is clear to me that you live in a modest townhouse in Holborn, and the immaculate condition of your shoes indicates that you travelled here by hansom cab. You have no children of your own, only a stepson from your husband's previous marriage".

The lady must have blinked in confusion, clearly taken aback by Holmes's assertions. "I'm afraid you are quite mistaken, Mr Holmes," she stammered. "I actually reside in a manor house, situated in Wimbledon on the outskirts of London. Moreover, I have two children, and my dear husband and I were betrothed as soon as we both came of age."

Holmes sounded momentarily nonplussed by Mrs. Worthington's correction, but he quickly regained his composure and continued with his investigation. "No matter, madam," he said dismissively, "Such details are ultimately of little consequence. The true matter at hand is the mysterious scene you discovered in your stables. I shall need to examine the premises post-haste."

With that, Holmes and Watson hastily prepared for their departure, leaving a bewildered Mrs. Worthington to go about her business. Watson packing his trusty service revolver. As they exited the building, I could not help but chuckle at the detective's latest display of folly. It seemed that, once again, I would need to employ my own considerable intellect to ensure the successful resolution of the case.

From my window, I observed the duo climbing into a hansom, and I decided to visit the Worthington residence later that day. As they disappeared from view, I knew that it would not be long before Holmes's bumbling missteps would provide me with yet another opportunity to steer him towards the truth.

In the meantime, I settled back into my chair, my thoughts turning to the gender-changing horse and sugar-cubes that Mrs. Worthington had described. What secrets could this mystery hold, and what dangers might lie ahead? As the sun reached its apex and the city buzzed with life beyond my window, I found myself eagerly anticipating the challenges and intrigues that awaited me in the future.

Several hours later, I observed Holmes and Watson returning to Baker Street, their expressions a mixture of excitement and confusion. Unable to resist the continuation of eavesdropping on their conversation, I pressed myself a glass against the adjoining wall, straining to catch every word.

"I tell you, Watson," Holmes exclaimed, "despite us finding nothing out of the ordinary, there is more to this case than meets the eye! The change in the horse's behaviour and the cubes of sugar are but pieces of an elaborate puzzle, designed to confound and deceive!" The sudden change of gender apparently not a remarkable clue.

Dr Watson, ever the voice of reason, replied cautiously, "But Holmes, surely it is more likely that we are dealing with a simple case of dementia, rather than some grand conspiracy?"

"Nonsense, Watson!" Holmes retorted, waving his pipe dismissively. "The facts clearly point to a far more complex and sinister scheme. I suspect that we have stumbled upon the machinations of an international cabal, plotting to destabilise the British government through a campaign of subterfuge and terror!"

As I listened to Holmes's absurd theories, I couldn't help but shake my head in bemusement. It seemed that, once again, the great detective had allowed his overactive imagination to lead him astray. Resolute in my determination to discover the truth, I began to prepare for my own investigation of the Worthington stables.

Donning an impeccable disguise as a mobile leatherworker, I made my way to the Worthington estate. As I approached the magnificent property, I was struck by the grandiosity of the scene that unfolded before me. The stables, resplendent in their architectural splendour, housed an impressive cavalcade of equine majesty, their noble steeds exhibiting the finest pedigree and conditioning. A panoply of riders, clad in the most exquisite equestrian attire, demonstrated their consummate horsemanship as they gracefully navigated the meticulously maintained paddocks, each movement executed with the precision and elegance of a well-rehearsed ballet.

The atmosphere was replete with the palpable excitement of the gymkhana, an equestrian competition designed to test the mettle and skill of both horse and rider. The verdant expanse of the estate grounds was punctuated by an array of obstacles and challenges, each meticulously arranged to provide a thorough examination of the competitors' prowess in the saddle. The fragrant scent of fresh hay and the invigorating aroma of well-groomed horses permeated the air, further underscoring the ambiance of equine excellence that pervaded the Worthington estate.

Upon my arrival, I was greeted by a flustered groom, who ushered me inside the property without question. Using my tools as my credentials, I swiftly gained access to the stable, where I began my meticulous examination of the horse and the surroundings.

The horse, it seemed, was an impressive steed. Having little experience with equine, I was unable to discern anything useful about the animal, except to verify that it was indeed a male, despite its official registration to the contrary. A simple glance provided the necessary evidence of gender.

Moving onto the stable, my gaze was inexorably drawn to a folded, partially torn fragment of parchment that lay nestled next to a single sugar-cube amongst the hay, as if accidentally dropped. On one corner, several dirty thumbprints, perhaps created by a grubby hand. The significance of this seemingly inconsequential discovery was not immediately apparent;

however, upon closer inspection, I discerned that it bore upon its surface a meticulously inscribed catalogue of names and dates, with a number of entries appearing to have been expeditiously effaced with a frenzied flourish of ink.

It dawned upon me with startling clarity that I had, quite fortuitously, happened upon a potentially invaluable piece of evidence which had, in all likelihood, eluded the typically perspicacious gaze of Mr Sherlock Holmes. In his eagerness to embrace his more outlandish and preposterous conjectures, it seemed that he had overlooked this crucial clue, which now lay nestled within the confines of my hand, a tantalising harbinger of revelations yet to come.

As I stood amidst the unmistakable aroma of the countryside, I pondered the circumstances which had led me to this moment. The reported change in the horse's demeanour; the carelessly dropped cubes of sugar; and by no means least, the enigmatic transmutation in the creature's gender.

With the evidence in hand, I made my way back to my own residence, eager to delve deeper into the mystery of the sugar-cubes and the altered beast. As I pored over the list of names, I felt the thrill of the hunt surge through my veins, and I knew that it was only a matter of time before I uncovered the truth.

Once again, it fell to me, Horatio Ollerenthorpe, to guide the bumbling Sherlock Holmes towards the resolution of the case, and to ensure that justice was served. For, in a world teeming with deception and intrigue, it was my unerring intuition and keen intellect that served as the silent bulwark against the forces of darkness.

As I scrutinised the list, I gradually began to discern a pattern. The individuals named were all wealthy horse owners domiciled within the regions around London, and the accompanying dates corresponded to the races in which their prized steeds were scheduled to compete. Mr Rex Worthington, the husband of Mrs Constance Worthington, featured at the very top of the list, his entry in the list crossed out. It appeared that the peculiar mystery of the horse, the sugar-cubes and the fragment of parchment were somehow connected to the world of horse racing and its attendant intrigue. Perhaps the other persons on the list had received a similar maleficent visit by person or persons unknown?

Realising the significance of this discovery, I knew that I must find a way to convey the list to Sherlock Holmes, lest his hare-brained theories continue to lead him further astray. And so, in the dead of night, I slipped the list under the door of 221B Baker Street, hoping that it would serve as a beacon of reason amidst the fog of Holmes's preposterous conjecture.

The following day, I listened with interest as Holmes excitedly showed the list to Dr Watson. However, rather than guiding him towards a more rational understanding of the case, the detective used the information to bolster his own wild theories.

"Ah, Watson!" Holmes ejaculated, brandishing the list in excitement. "This document confirms my suspicions! The international cabal I spoke of is, in fact, a shadowy organisation that seeks to control the world of horse racing for their own foul purposes! They have infiltrated the highest echelons of British society, and it is our duty to expose their insidious plot!"

I could scarcely believe my ears as I listened to Holmes's fantastical interpretation of the evidence. It seemed that no amount of guidance would be sufficient to counteract his penchant for the absurd. Nevertheless, I continued to listen as the detective embarked on his misguided quest for the truth.

Having established their course of action, Holmes donned a series of ludicrous disguises, each more preposterous than the last. Later describing his first visit, he had dressed as a flamboyant French jockey, replete with a garish silk cravat and an extravagantly waxed moustache. He presented himself at the home of Sir Reginald Fitzroy, one of the prominent horse owners on the list, and proceeded to engage the bewildered gentleman in a nonsensical conversation about equine dentistry and other irrelevant topics.

With a ridiculous accent and a laughable outfit, he strode into the drawing-room, where Sir Reginald was enjoying a cup of tea.

"Ah, bonjour, Sir Reginald!" Holmes exclaimed in a heavily exaggerated French accent. "I am François Duvalier, ze jockey extraordinaire! I 'ave come to discuss ze finer points of 'orse racing with you."

Sir Reginald, bemused by the sudden appearance of this peculiar character, raised an eyebrow but decided to play along. "Ah, Monsieur Duvalier, a pleasure to meet you. I am quite fond of the sport, having a stable full of my own thoroughbreds, though I must say I've never heard of you."

Holmes, not one to be deterred by Sir Reginald's scepticism, proceeded to engage in a meandering conversation about horse racing that had little, if any, connection to the matter at hand. As they spoke of trifling details such as the weather, the quality of the turf, and the merits of various riding techniques, it became increasingly clear that Holmes was failing to direct the conversation towards the list of names.

Eventually, Holmes mustered the courage to broach the subject, albeit in a roundabout manner. "Sir Reginald," he began, still in his exaggerated accent, "I 'ave 'eard rumours zat you may 'ave been ze victim of a mysterious event about your stables recently?"

Sir Reginald, who had been humouring Holmes up until this point, now appeared genuinely puzzled. "I'm afraid I have no idea what you're talking about, Monsieur Duvalier. There has been no incident of note on my property."

Holmes, realising that his absurd ruse had failed to produce any useful information, decided to beat a hasty retreat. "Ah, I see. Well, it must 'ave been a mistake. Excusez-moi for wasting your time, Sir Reginald. Au revoir!"

With that, Holmes made his exit, leaving Sir Reginald to no doubt ponder the strange encounter he had just experienced. Needless to say, Holmes gleaned no useful information from this encounter, and he returned to Baker Street to prepare for his next interview.

Holmes, having failed miserably in his previous attempt to extract information from Sir Reginald Fitzroy, decided to don a new disguise, this time as a monocled Prussian horse breeder. He hoped this change would have allowed him to successfully uncover the connection between Lady Delilah Harrington and the mysterious list of names found inside Mrs Worthington's stables.

Adopting a thick Prussian accent and dressing in the attire of a well-to-do horse breeder, Holmes had arrived at Lady Delilah's country residence, ready to launch into another seemingly pointless conversation. Upon entering the drawing room, he bowed deeply and introduced himself, "Guten tag, Lady Delilah. Mein name ist Herr Otto von Himmelreich, und I am a distinguished horse breeder from Prussia."

Lady Delilah, a woman of considerable social standing, had eyed Holmes with suspicion but decided to entertain his visit. "Mr von Himmelreich, how intriguing. I do have an interest in horses, but I must confess I've never heard of you."

Undeterred by Lady Delilah's uncertainty, Holmes had delved into a lengthy discussion on the intricacies of horse breeding, describing the virtues of various Prussian breeds and the importance of bloodlines. Yet, once again, the conversation strayed far from the matter at hand.

Finally, Holmes attempted to steer the dialogue towards the list of names. "Lady Delilah," he began in his Prussian accent, "I have recently come across some interesting information that suggests you may have been a victim of unwanted ingress into your property. Is that so?"

Lady Delilah raised an eyebrow and appeared genuinely confused. "Mr von Himmelreich, I must say I have absolutely no idea what you are talking about. I advise you to authenticate your sources of information."

Holmes, realising that his ludicrous disguise and irrelevant conversation had once again failed to uncover any pertinent information, decided to take his leave. "Ah, I apologise for any confusion, Lady Delilah. I must have been mistaken. Auf wiedersehen!"

With a theatrical click of the heels and a swift exit, Holmes left in his wake Lady Delilah to ponder what can only be described as a bizarre encounter. Despite the utter farce of Holmes's investigations, neither Sir Reginald nor Lady Delilah revealed anything of substance concerning the case. It seemed that the great detective's imbecility had, once again, led him down a blind alley, leaving the true nature of the conspiracy shrouded in mystery.

However, I remained undeterred in my pursuit of the truth, confident that my own keen intellect and steely determination would ultimately uncover the secrets that lay hidden beneath the surface of the Worthington affair. And so, as Holmes continued to flounder in the murky depths of his own folly, it was clear that I soon had to embark on a new course of investigation, one that would lead me ever closer to the heart of the conspiracy and the shadowy figures who sought to manipulate the world of horse racing for their own execrable ends.

Undaunted by his previous failures, Holmes persisted in his quixotic quest to interview the remaining individuals on the list. For his third visit, he had assumed the identity of an eccentric Italian horse trainer, complete with an outrageous wig of curly black hair and a bushy moustache that would have been the envy of any operatic baritone. In this outlandish guise, he had called upon Mr Michael Beaumont, another prominent horse owner, and proceeded to demonstrate his purported skills in equine physiotherapy. Despite Holmes's enthusiastic ministrations, Mr Beaumont remained tight-lipped, providing no insights into the case.

For the fourth visit, Holmes transformed himself into a Russian horse whisperer, resplendent in a fur hat and a long, flowing beard that threatened to engulf his entire face. Presenting himself at the residence of Mrs. Henrietta Cavendish, he regaled her with tales of his alleged adventures in the wilds of Siberia, training the legendary Tunguska racehorses. Yet, once again, the interview yielded no useful information, leaving Holmes no closer to understanding the nature of the mystery.

Undeterred, Holmes embarked on his fifth visit, adopting the persona of a Scottish farrier with a penchant for composing horse-themed poetry. Donning a kilt and a shock of flaming red hair, he appeared on the doorstep of Lord Algernon Fitzwilliam, reciting his original verses with great gusto. Despite Holmes's impassioned performance, Lord Fitzwilliam appeared more bemused than enlightened, offering no pertinent details about the case.

For the sixth visit, Holmes assumed the role of an American horse dealer, preposterously clad in a Stetson hat and a pair of ostentatiously embroidered cowboy boots. He swaggered into the home of Lady Constance Cholmondeley, regaling her with tales of his supposed exploits on the dusty plains of Texas. Yet, as with his previous interviews, Holmes's theatrics bore no fruit, leaving the detective empty-handed and no closer to the truth.

Listening to their fireside recount of these farcical visits, I couldn't help but grimace at the incredulity and sheer absurdity of Holmes's tactics. It seemed that the hapless detective was utterly blind to the glaringly obvious, his boundless imagination and propensity for the fantastical obstructing his path to the truth. And so, as Holmes continued to stumble from one comical misadventure to another, I resolved to continue my own investigation, confident that my unerring intuition and keen intellect would ultimately bring some clarity to the shadowy threat to the chaotic world of horse racing.

The next morning, I overheard Holmes informing Watson of his intention to visit the final name on the list, the only one left uncrossed. Watson, showing a glimmer of sense, inquired why Holmes had left this particular individual for last, rather than commencing his inquiries there.

Holmes, ever the master of ridicule, responded with a convoluted explanation. "Ah, Watson, it is a matter of strategic cunning! You see, our adversaries, being the sly foxes that they are, would expect us to begin with the most obvious lead. Thus, by visiting the least likely horse owners first, we have lulled our quarry into a false sense of security, thereby rendering them ripe for the picking!"

Watson nodded in bemused agreement, clearly unable to penetrate the fog of Holmes's delusions. And so, the detective set out on his final visit, this time disguised as a Spanish horse veterinarian, complete with a luxuriant wig of flowing black locks and a cape embroidered with the image of a rearing stallion.

Upon arriving at the residence of the mysterious final name, however, Holmes had discovered that the house and outbuildings were entirely empty. Not a stick of furniture remained, as if the occupants had vanished into thin air. Rather than drawing any useful conclusions from this curious state of affairs, Holmes had merely scratched his head in befuddlement and returned to Baker

Street, his investigation once again stymied by his own obtuseness.

Unable to endure this farce any longer, I resolved to visit the empty house myself, confident that my keen powers of observation would reveal the clues that had eluded the hapless Holmes. Slipping into the shadows, I made my way to the abandoned residence and let myself in through a rear door that showed obvious signs of previous entry procured by hobnail boots.

The interior of the house was as barren as Holmes had described, the walls stripped of their ornamentation and the floors bereft of even a single scrap of carpet, their only adornment was an occasionally discarded sugar-cube. Yet, as I prowled through the echoing chambers, my sharp eyes detected something that the great detective had overlooked: another small scrap of paper, singed by flame on all but one side, half-hidden between dusty floorboards. Upon closer examination, I realised that the scrap bore the faint imprint of a series of numbers and letters, as if it had once been part of a larger document.

Convinced that this new fragment held the key to the entire mystery, I pocketed the scrap and returned to my own lodgings, determined to decipher its cryptic contents. As I settled down to my task, I could hear Holmes and Watson in the adjoining room, still blathering on about their wild theories and nonsensical conjectures.

I could not help but feel a mixture of pity and contempt for the frustrating duo, their minds forever ensnared or complicit in the tangled web of Holmes' misguided fantasies. And so, as they continued to flounder in the murky depths of their delusions, I pressed on with my own investigation, sure-footed that my unerring intuition and superior intellect would ultimately lead me to the truth and bring the shadowy conspirators to justice.

Decoding the cryptic message on the scrap of paper proved to be a challenge, but I soon discovered that the series of numbers and letters were, in fact, a cryptogram of ingenious makeup. Utilising my considerable intellect and perspicacity, I embarked upon the intricate task of deciphering the enigmatic code.

Upon closer inspection, I discerned a pattern in the cipher, suggesting that the characters might have been obfuscated using a polyalphabetic substitution method. To ascertain whether my hypothesis held water, I endeavoured to employ the venerable Vigenère cipher, a cryptographic system that had been the bane of codebreakers for centuries.

With steadfast determination and meticulous precision, I began the laborious process of constructing a Vigenère table, a vital instrument in the decryption of this enciphered conundrum. Utilising a probable key, I aligned the rows and columns of the table to unravel the complex interplay of shifting alphabets. As the decryption progressed, a distinct message began to coalesce from the jumbled morass of characters.

My efforts were rewarded when the obfuscated text resolved into a comprehensible series of letters, revealing the details of the crime, a location, and a date. It became clear that the felons were intent on switching out the favourite horses in the upcoming Gold Cup, resulting in the fixing of the race and the pocketing of a considerable gambling purse. The pieces of this confounding puzzle now fell into place, elucidating the mysterious occurrences within the Worthington stables!

I surmised that the location and date pointed to a clandestine rendezvous, the epicentre of the malefactors' criminal machinations. The coordinates pointed to a stable situated in a suburb of London, and the date indicated that a potentially sinister plot would be set in motion that very evening.

Eureka! The revelation was both invigorating and disquieting. It was now incumbent upon me to devise an ingenious stratagem to thwart any wrongdoers and preserve the integrity of the Gold Cup. Holmes, in his characteristic fatuity, had hitherto proven to be of little assistance. It was with a heavy heart and steely resolve that I prepared to confront the criminals orchestrating the well organised swindle.

Realising the urgency of the situation, I decided to act swiftly. I scribbled a carefully worded message hinting at the deciphered location and date, slipping it into an envelope addressed to Sherlock Holmes. I then posted it through his letterbox, hoping that, for once, he might take heed of the evidence laid before him.

As luck would have it, Holmes and Watson were amid another fruitless debate over their outlandish theories when my missive arrived. The sudden arrival of the envelope piqued their curiosity, and they eagerly tore it open, devouring the contents with a mixture of surprise and confusion.

In their sitting room, Holmes and Watson engaged in a preposterous disquisition that demonstrated their lack of discernment. Holmes, with his customary pomposity, expounded upon an implausible hypothesis involving a secret society of international anarchists' intent on subverting the very foundations of the British Empire. Watson, ever the credulous accomplice, listened with rapt attention and pen in hand, punctuating Holmes's bombastic soliloquy with exclamations of wonderment and awe.

Holmes pontificated at length, employing the most grandiloquent language and tortuous reasoning to bolster his convoluted conjecture. He regaled Watson with an elaborate narrative of political intrigue, clandestine machinations, and nefarious double-dealing, all seemingly corroborated by the flimsiest of evidence. Watson, in his inimitable fashion, expressed both astonishment and admiration for his friend's ostensible acumen.

As the outlandish conversation continued, I could not help but marvel at the absurdity of their discourse. Holmes' penchant for finding conspiracies in the most mundane of circumstances had evidently led him far astray in this instance. It was with a mixture of amusement and frustration that I observed their futile intellectual meanderings.

Finally, their circuitous deliberations reached an end, and Holmes and Watson set out for the location I had furnished. Their eagerness to uncover the truth, albeit misguided, was palpable. Disguising myself with my usual cunning, I trailed the pair, intent on witnessing first-hand the denouement of this extraordinary adventure.

As Holmes and Watson stealthily approached the stable, the rich aroma of manure assaulted their delicate nostrils. Through handkerchiefs held firmly over their noses, they engaged in a muffled, ludicrous discussion, attempting to reconcile their preposterous theories with the reality of the situation at hand. Holmes, ever the self-assured cretin, persisted in his belief that a vast international conspiracy lurked behind every corner, while Watson, good-natured and compliant when requisite, nodded in agreement.

The pair's conversation was replete with abstruse terminology, obfuscating the facts with a fog of verbosity. Holmes propounded his outlandish theory that the horse-switching plot was but a single cog in a much larger machine, one designed to destabilise the Empire's economy and thereby sow the seeds of chaos throughout the realm. Watson, barely swayed by his companion's ostentatious erudition, offered exclamations of amazement and veneration.

As they patiently waited for action, Holmes and Watson peered through the slats of the stable door. Their discourse meandered through a thicket of hypotheses, each more improbable than the last. Holmes, determined to maintain his reputation as a master of deduction, sought to weave together the disparate strands of evidence into a coherent narrative. Watson, meanwhile, alternated between supporting his friend's wild conjectures and offering his own more grounded interpretations of the events unfolding before them.

As the duo engaged in their convoluted deliberations, their attentions were fortuitously drawn to a pair of furtive miscreants who, unbeknownst to them, were in the very act of exchanging one equine for another. The ruffians, evidently confident in the success of their criminal subterfuge, conducted their business with an air of brazen audacity, scarcely bothering to conceal their illicit activities from the prying eyes of the unsuspecting pair.

Emboldened by the prospect of apprehending the culprits and, in so doing, unveiling the true nature of their criminal machinations, Holmes and Watson leapt precipitously into the fray, their valour overshadowing any notion of caution or self-preservation. Alas, their impetuous zeal was met with swift and brutal resistance, as the two malefactors, emboldened by their villainous intent, set upon the hapless duo with unbridled ferocity.

Holmes' lanky frame whirled confusingly in a bartitsu *kata*. Ill-suited to the rigours of physical combat, he was swiftly incapacitated by a thunderous blow to the cranium, his erstwhile opponent displaying an unnerving proficiency in the pugilistic arts. Watson, meanwhile, despite his military training and a valiant display of martial prowess, found himself similarly overwhelmed by the relentless onslaught of his brutish adversary. The taller of the degenerate pair retrieved a curved, keen-edged blade from a concealed compartment within his waistcoat, his countenance replete with malice and determination. Positioned menacingly, he prepared to sever the necks of his defeated foes.

With the situation growing increasingly dire and the prospect of a calamitous denouement looming ever larger, I determined that it was incumbent upon myself to intervene in the proceedings, lest our intrepid heroes succumb to the depredations of their assailants. Ensconced within the shadows, I surreptitiously armed myself with a humble peashooter, my weapon of choice in this most unorthodox of skirmishes.

Taking quick but careful aim, I discharged my projectile at the rump of the steed closest to the action, a magnificent specimen of equine splendour whose hindquarters presented an irresistible target for my unerring marksmanship. The effect of this seemingly innocuous intervention was nothing short of miraculous, as the startled beast, its equanimity shattered by the sudden sting of the peashooter's impact, lashed out with a devastating kick.

The force of the horse's retaliatory manoeuvre was sufficient to incapacitate the two miscreants, sugar-cubes spilling from the pocket of the younger of the pair, their villainous countenances contorted in expressions of shock and dismay as they crumpled to the ground, rendered unconscious by the sheer might of the equine's wrath. With their adversaries thus neutralised, Holmes and Watson were free to extricate themselves from their precarious predicament, albeit with a modicum of embarrassment at their unceremonious defeat.

As they picked themselves up from the dust, brushing aside the detritus of their ill-fated encounter, the duo exchanged a series of bemused and silent glances, attempting to make sense of the bewildering turn of events that had transpired. Never one to forgo an opportunity to indulge, Watson stooped to retrieve a solitary sugar-cube from the ground, strewn with hay and other organic matter. With due care, he proceeded to wipe the morsel upon the lapel of his ulster, subsequently introducing it into his eagerly waiting orifice, his eyebrows arching in an unmistakable display of delectation.

"Mmmm," his only utterance.

Holmes, ever the consummate raconteur, began to expound upon a tortuous explanation for their unexpected reprieve, attributing their salvation to his own fruitless display of martial arts, or perhaps even the machinations of providence itself.

Watson proceeded to shake his head in bewilderment, offering his own conjectures as to the nature of their mysterious emancipation, all the while studiously avoiding any mention of their ignominious defeat at the hands of the brutish miscreants. Little did they know that their deliverance had been orchestrated by none other than myself, a humble observer whose unobtrusive presence had, by a fortuitous combination of circumstance and ingenuity, served to extricate them from the jaws of certain doom.

At long last, their conversation was interrupted by the arrival of the police, whom I had discreetly summoned to the scene. The officers stormed the stable, taking the astonished criminals into custody. Holmes and Watson, their faces a mixture of shock and triumph, emerged from their hiding place to witness the denouement of their misadventure.

In the aftermath of the arrests, Holmes and Watson engaged in yet another preposterous debate, this time concerning the true motivations of the culprits and the implications of their actions for the Empire at large. Oblivious to the fact that their success had been orchestrated by my unseen hand, the pair congratulated themselves on their deductive prowess and vowed to remain ever vigilant in defence of Queen and country.

The gratitude of Mrs Constance Worthington was a flowing as her skirts. With the crime solved, Holmes and Watson were invited to myriad social events to toast their success, celebrating their cunning and genius amongst the societal elite.

Thus, concluded yet another escapade of the inimitable Sherlock Holmes and his trusty sidekick, Dr John Watson, their farcical investigations serving as a constant source of amusement for those fortunate enough to observe their antics from behind the scenes.

And so, as I reflected upon the case from the comfort my own lodgings, I resolved to continue my secret vigil, ever watchful for the next opportunity to steer my bumbling neighbour towards the truth. For, in the end, it was not the genius of Sherlock Holmes that protected the citizens of London, but the quiet, unassuming figure who observed the infamous detective from his window, armed with nothing but his keen intellect and an unwavering determination to see justice done.

Chapter 5: The Case of the Rival Inventors

It was a blustery autumn day when I observed the arrival of a new client at the doorstep of 221B Baker Street. From the window of my residence, I could see the figure of a tall, slender gentleman, dressed in a fine frock coat and sporting a neatly trimmed beard. The urgency in his gait suggested that his purpose was of a most pressing nature.

Upon entering the rooms of the Sherlock Holmes, the client introduced himself as Mr Edwin Smythe, an inventor of some renown. He had recently patented a ground-breaking device, which he claimed would revolutionise the burgeoning field of electrical engineering. However, he had received word that his designs were in danger of being stolen by a rival inventor, a certain Mr Marcel Merquin, who had long harboured a grudge against him. Several attempts of a theft had since been detected, thwarted by a most secure locked safe, yet Smythe remained certain that Merquin's endeavour would eventually succeed.

Holmes, never one to let an opportunity for grandiosity slip through his fingers, leapt to his feet, and began to examine Mr Smythe with his customary zeal. "Ah, my dear sir," he declared, "I perceive that you hail from the East End of London, and that you arrived here by means of a hansom cab, drawn by a horse with a slight limp in its left foreleg. You are a fan of the exotic Italian food, indicated by the faint aroma of Mediterranean herbs."

Mr Smythe stared at Holmes in astonishment, clearly baffled by the detective's pronouncements. "Well, that's quite incorrect, Mr Holmes," he said with a bemused smile. "I actually live in Kensington, and I walked here this morning, having taken the omnibus as far as Piccadilly. As for the aroma, it is simply hand soap."

Holmes, rather than admitting his error, merely sniffed disdainfully and dismissed the abrupt rebuttal. "No matter, no matter," he muttered, "the particulars of your journey are of little consequence. Pray, continue with your tale."

As Mr Smythe recounted the details of his predicament, I listened intently from my vantage point, making mental notes of the salient points. It seemed that Merquin had long coveted Smythe's inventions and had been implicated in a series of industrial espionage incidents in the past. The threat to Smythe's latest patent was therefore a grave concern, for the loss of his designs could spell financial ruin for the beleaguered inventor.

Throughout the conversation, Holmes appeared to be only half-listening, his attention audibly wandering, as if bored by the gentleman. He occasionally interjected with a question or comment, invariably displaying a profound misunderstanding of the matter at hand.

At one point, he asked Mr Smythe if he had considered the possibility that the theft was an inside job, perpetrated by one of his own employees. Smythe, growing increasingly exasperated, replied that he had no employees, as he conducted all his research in the solitude of his personal laboratory. Holmes merely nodded sagely, as if this revelation somehow confirmed his own theories.

As the interview drew to a close, I could hear that Mr Smythe was growing increasingly sceptical of Holmes's abilities. Yet, with no other recourse, he reluctantly agreed to entrust the case to the bumbling detective, who promised to leave no stone unturned in his pursuit of the truth.

Upon the conclusion of their interview with the apprehensive Mr Smythe, Holmes and Watson, with characteristic alacrity, endeavoured to delve into the intricacies of the case. Their minds abuzz with a cacophony of fantastical conjectures, they embarked upon an animated discourse, oblivious to the manifest absurdity of their ruminations.

"Ah, Watson," Holmes began, his voice redolent with the inordinate zeal that so often heralded the commencement of his investigations, "this case presents a cornucopia of enigmas and conundrums, a bewildering labyrinth of possibilities that demands our most assiduous attention. I propose that we commence our inquiries by examining the social circles frequented by the rival inventor, for it is within these rarefied environs that we shall doubtless unearth the clues that shall guide us to the heart of this most perplexing matter."

Watson, his countenance suffused with an air of bemused indulgence, nodded slowly at his companion's words, offering a theory of his own as he stroked his moustache in contemplation. "Indeed, Holmes, I concur that our quarry may be found lurking amidst the shadows of high society. It is entirely possible that the perpetrator of these atrocious deeds is a member of some clandestine cabal, a sinister conclave of ne'er-do-wells and evildoers who conspire to perpetrate their dastardly crimes beneath the very noses of the unsuspecting populace."

Holmes, his eyes alight with the flames of intrigue, clapped his hands together in exuberant approval of Watson's hypothesis. "Capital, my dear Watson! A clandestine cabal, you say? That is precisely the sort of insidious organisation that would be capable of orchestrating such a confounding series of events. Make sure to write that down, there's a good chap. We must delve into the seamy underbelly of our fair city, casting aside the veil of propriety and decorum to expose the festering malignancies that lurk within."

As the two detectives continued to expound upon their outlandish suppositions, their voices growing ever more fervent and impassioned, it became increasingly apparent that they were venturing further and further afield from the true nature of the case. They spoke of arcane rituals and secret pacts, of purloined artefacts and coded missives, weaving a tangled web of conjecture and speculation that bore little resemblance to the genuine state of affairs.

And yet, for all their wild theorising and fantastical flights of fancy, the duo seemed utterly convinced of the veracity of their deductions, their misguided confidence unshaken by the glaring absence of any semblance of reason or logic. Indeed, as their conversation reached its zealous crescendo, it was difficult to discern whether their enthusiasm was borne of genuine insight or merely the product of Holmes' own self-aggrandising delusions and storytelling. To the discerning observer, their impassioned discourse appeared more akin to the fevered imaginings of overwrought minds than the sober deliberations of seasoned investigators.

I sighed in resignation, knowing that it would once again fall to me to save the day. For, while Holmes might blunder and bluster his way through the investigation, I had no doubt that my own powers of deduction would be more than equal to the task at hand.

And so, with a steely determination in my heart, I set about my own inquiries, my keen mind already probing the depths of the mystery that lay before me. Taking the obvious first step in any rationally planned investigation, I resolved to visit Mr Smythe's laboratory in Kensington first, under the pretext of being a potential investor, to gather any information that might prove useful.

As I approached the abode of Mr Smythe, I was immediately struck by its peculiar and incongruous appearance. The facade, though clearly of a considerable age, was adorned with an array of curious contraptions and mechanical devices, the purpose of which remained inscrutable to the casual observer. From the street, the dwelling appeared to be a veritable sanctuary for the inquisitive and intellectually inclined, its interior walls lined with voluminous tomes that bespoke a voracious appetite for knowledge and the pursuit of erudition.

Instead of the usual ornate brass door knocker, a solitary button was the only object to adorn the old, oak door. Taking a chance, I proceeded to tentatively push the button, and I subsequently heard the unmistakable sound of a gong, emanating from deep within the edifice. After a short delay, the door slowly creaked open and I was greeted by the nervous smile of Mr Smythe.

With open arms, I introduced myself. "Good day Mr Smythe! I am Mr Victor Fassbender. I believe you are expecting me?" Met by a polite nod and a flourish of the arm, I was invited to enter and follow him inside.

Upon crossing the threshold, I found myself ensconced within an atmosphere of frenetic creativity, the air redolent with the scent of oil and solder, as well as the unmistakable aroma of intellectual endeavour. The domicile was a veritable labyrinth of curiosities, its cluttered confines overflowing with experimental apparatus and half-finished contrivances. In one corner stood a prodigious assortment of clockwork automata, their intricate mechanisms ticking away in a symphony of industry, while in another lay a most unusual variant of a gramophone, its gears and cogs whirring with an almost preternatural precision.

"That is my Regamautophone," Smythe explained, noting my interest in the gramophone. "It offers unrivalled audio clarity."

"I expect it does," I replied, without any comprehension of Smythe's meaning to back my statement up. In addition, I felt an inexplicable sense of pre-cognition, but I quickly brushed it aside.

Throughout the dwelling, one could not help but feel a sense of disarray, a palpable aura of disorder that seemed to both mirror and amplify the chaotic nature of Mr Smythe's inventive spirit. And yet, amidst the apparent disorganisation, there was an undeniable sense of purpose and ingenuity that permeated the very air, a testament to the boundless creativity that held sway over the domicile's occupant.

As we navigated the cluttered chambers, I was struck by the sheer profusion of unconventional and experimental machinery that adorned the premises. A peculiar contraption designed to brew the perfect cup of tea stood proudly upon a dishevelled sideboard, its myriad tubes and valves emanating a faint hiss of steam as they whirred and clanked in harmonious cacophony. Elsewhere, a seemingly innocuous set of bookshelves revealed itself to be an ingenious system of interlocking gears and pulleys, each tome connected to a hidden mechanism that allowed the entire structure to pivot and swivel, granting access to yet more volumes secreted within the walls themselves.

Indeed, every corner of Mr Smythe's abode was a testament to the boundless potential of the human mind and the relentless drive to explore the uncharted realms of possibility. It was a dwelling that embodied the very essence of Victorian ingenuity and the indefatigable spirit of discovery, a microcosm of the age in which it stood.

As he led me through the workshop, explaining the intricacies of his device, I carefully scrutinised every nook and cranny, searching for any clue that might hint at foul play. Upon reaching the laboratory, after further pleasantries, Smythe eagerly demonstrated his latest invention to whom he believed was a prospective patron.

It was during this tour that I noticed a curious set of bi-directional footprints, partially concealed beneath a layer of dust and iron filings. The prints were small, suggesting a person of diminutive stature. They led between a large portrait in an ornate frame on the wall, and a hidden door at the back of the workshop. I made a mental note of this discovery, knowing that it might prove crucial in unravelling the tangled web of intrigue that surrounded the case.

Upon completing my inspection of the workshop, I turned to Mr Smythe, my countenance carefully composed so as to belie the significance of the discovery I had just made. "Mr Smythe," I began, my voice suffused with an air of diplomacy, "I must confess that, whilst your invention is doubtless a marvel of modern ingenuity, I fear that it is not quite suited to my particular proclivities and requirements."

Smythe, his visage a picture of crestfallen disappointment, appeared momentarily bereft of words, as though he had been struck a grievous blow. Sensing his dejection, I hastened to offer some manner of consolation, my words carefully chosen to instil a sense of hope and optimism.

"However," I continued, my tone taking on a more sanguine and reassuring quality, "I have a number of acquaintances and confederates within the metropolis who I am certain would be most eager to seize the opportunity to provide financial patronage for the development and refinement of your ingenious contrivance. I would be more than willing to make the requisite introductions and facilitate the establishment of a mutually beneficial partnership."

At these words, Mr Smythe's countenance brightened considerably, his initial disappointment supplanted by a renewed sense of hope and enthusiasm. Thus mollified, he expressed his gratitude for my offer, little suspecting that my true motivations lay elsewhere. And with that, I left the abode of Mr Smythe and redirected my attention to discovering the identity of the thwarted intruder.

As I persevered in my pursuit of the truth, I delved into the murky depths of the criminal underworld and utilising my own unique skillset to navigate the labyrinthine network of informants and ne'er-do-wells that populated this sordid realm. After several hours of dogged investigation, I gradually began to weave together a more cohesive and cogent narrative of the events that had unfolded.

My inquiries led me down a multitude of winding paths, each lined with the shadows and secrets of the city's most elusive denizens. It was within the dimly lit recesses of a disreputable public house that I chanced upon an acquaintance of dubious repute, a man whom I had cultivated as an informant during my many years spent navigating the treacherous waters of the criminal underworld. His moniker, "Whispering Willie," was an apt reflection of his propensity for acquiring and disseminating information of the most confidential and sensitive nature. Ensconced within a darkened corner of the smoke-filled establishment, our conversation was conducted in hushed tones, the air heavy with the weight of secrets yet to be divulged.

"Willie," I began, my voice scarcely more than a murmur, "I find myself in dire need of your assistance. It has come to my attention that a certain individual by the name of Merquin has most likely enlisted the services of a master thief in order to acquire certain documents from a Mr Edwin Smythe residing somewhere in Kensington. I beseech you, sir, to share with me any information you might possess concerning this nefarious alliance, for it is of the utmost import that I uncover the truth behind their maleficent machinations."

Two sovereigns were proffered under the table into my companion's clammy hand. "There are two more of those, if your information meets my requirement," I promised with a whisper. After snatching the coins, Whispering Willie's eyes darted about the room with the habitual caution of a man forever wary of unseen eavesdroppers. He seemed to weigh the risks and rewards of divulging the information I sought.

After a protracted silence that threatened to stretch into eternity, he finally spoke, his voice barely audible amidst the cacophony of raucous laughter and japery that filled the air.

"'Right as rain," he muttered, his voice barely more than a breath of Old Father Thames as he moved in, his mouth stinking of tobacco and gin. "I've heard whispers 'bout a little understandin' between your Merquin and a tea-leaf who goes by the name of 'The Rat'. The full picture's all sixes and sevens, and the straight dope harder to find than a sober toff at a boozer. The Rat's like a bloomin' ghost, an expert at ducking and diving and only a few bods know who he really is. Looks like Merquin was on his uppers enough to go look for this faceless bloke and ask him to pinch Smythe's most cherished designs."

Whispering Willie took a moment, throwing a surreptitious look around the room before continuing. "The word is that The Rat, with his sharp as a tack mind, sussed out a secret door in the walls of Smythe's workshop, a sneaky way in to make off with Smythe's precious secrets without anyone being the wiser. I don't know much more about their doings, the tracks gone all pear-shaped and the dark's creeping in. Knowin' the reputation of The Rat, all I can guess is their dodgy deal's worked out, and the fruits of their wrongdoings are now safe and sound in Merquin's mitts."

As the final words of Whispering Willie's revelation hung heavy in the air, I found myself filled with a renewed sense of purpose and determination. The threads of the tangled web I had been painstakingly unravelling had begun to coalesce, revealing a tapestry of deception and intrigue that stretched far beyond the scope of Holmes's and Watson's investigation. It was incumbent upon me to delve deeper into the shadows, to pursue the elusive spectre of The Rat and the enigmatic Merquin until the truth was laid bare and the full extent of their dastardly tactics exposed.

With a curt nod of gratitude, and after pressing two additional sovereigns into a waiting hand, I bade Whispering Willie farewell, leaving him to the whispers and furtive glances that were his stock in trade. As I strode forth from the dim and fetid confines of the public house, the cold night air serving as a stark contrast to the oppressive atmosphere within, I could not help but ponder the dire ramifications of the information I had gleaned from my recent discourse. The revelation of Merquin's involvement with the enigmatic figure known as The Rat had added a new layer of complexity to an already intricate tapestry of deceit. It seemed that the deeper I ventured into this labyrinth of secrets and lies, the more convoluted and perplexing the narrative became.

I was impelled to delve deep into the shadowy recesses of London's criminal underworld, a cunning web of vice and villainy, which stood in stark contrast to the genteel veneer of polite society. I resolved to consult with one Erasmus Trent, a man of dubious repute who was known to possess a wealth of knowledge concerning the schemes of the city's larcenist industry It was my fervent hope that this disreputable informant would provide me with the necessary information to unmask the elusive criminal known as The Rat.

I traversed the murky byways and winding alleys of London's East End, carefully cloaked in the disguise of an itinerant worker to avoid arousing suspicion. Upon arriving at yet another squalid public house, one that served as Trent's preferred haunt, I cautiously navigated the dimly lit interior, pausing to assess the motley assortment of patrons who frequented this den of iniquity. I observed cut-throats, women of ill-repute, and other patrons that were most likely both.

Spying Trent settled in a dark corner, I weaved my way through the malignant throng. As I approached the booth where Trent was ensconced, I noted the glint of cunning in his eyes, which bespoke a shrewd intellect lurking beneath his dishevelled appearance.

"G'd evenin', Trent," I began, "I'm 'ere seekin' enlightenment on a matter of grea' import. I 'spect that you are amenable to providin' me with the requisite knowledge in exchange for a gen'rous remuneration?"

Trent eyed me warily, the corners of his mouth twisting into a sardonic grin as he replied, "Well now, ain't you a fancy one? I reckon I might be able to provide you with the information you seek, but it'll cost you a pretty penny."

With a cautious sideways glance, I proffered the agreed-upon sum, noting with satisfaction the glint of greed that flashed across Trent's countenance as he eagerly pocketed the coins. He leaned in closer, his voice barely audible above the din of the public house, and began to divulge the secrets of The Rat's true identity.

"Your quarry, guv'nor, is a man by the name of Samuel Wilkes. By day, he plies his trade as a skilled locksmith, providing an honest service to the good people of London. But by night, he becomes The Rat, burglar for hire, employing his expertise to gain entry to the homes of the city's wealthiest toffs, relieving them of their valuable possessions to order, with skill and alacrity."

I listened intently as Trent elaborated upon Wilkes' tragic circumstances, detailing the desperate plight of his ailing wife and destitute children, which had driven this once-honourable man to embrace a life of crime. With each carefully chosen word, the true portrait of The Rat began to coalesce in my mind, a tragic figure driven to the brink of desperation by the cruel vicissitudes of fate. Finally, Trent completed his chronicle with the location of The Rat's base of operation in the bowels of Bow, a locale with a reputation for villainy and violent crime.

Eager to take my leave, I bid Trent a curt farewell, my heart heavy with the weight of my discoveries. Upon my return to Baker Street, I composed a missive detailing the results of my investigation. I surreptitiously conveyed the letter to Holmes, confident that he would utilise the information to bring The Rat to justice, whilst also ensuring that the unfortunate Wilkes family would receive the assistance they so desperately required.

As I located myself by my window, Holmes was at that very moment regaling Watson with yet another of his preposterous theories, which involved a cabal of disgruntled patent clerks and an elaborate conspiracy to undermine the British Empire. The arrival of my missive, however, quickly brought this flight of fancy to a crashing halt.

Holmes, upon reading the message, was momentarily silenced, his brow audibly furrowing in consternation. Then, with a triumphant cry, he leapt to his feet, exclaiming that he had cracked the case. Their ensuing conversation, replete with grandiose conjectures and fantastical hypotheses, was a constant stream of preposterousness, as they explored every possibility from the burglar being a member of the aristocracy to an agent of a foreign power.

Equipped with at least a workable theory and my tangible evidence, Holmes and Watson set out, revolvers secreted amongst their clothing, with myself disguised in their shadow, to apprehend The Rat, their sense of purpose renewed by the tantalising prospect of bringing the elusive criminal to justice. They traversed the fog-shrouded streets of London, their footfalls muffled by the damp cobblestones, as they made their way to the burglar's secret lair, hidden in plain sight amidst the bustling metropolis.

Upon arriving at the designated location in Bow, on a dank corner of Fairfield Road, Holmes and Watson paused to confer, their voices hushed by the gravity of their mission. They stood beneath a flickering gas lamp, its feeble glow casting eerie shadows upon the cobblestone street.

Holmes, his countenance alight with the feverish glow of inspiration, suggested an absurd stratagem to infiltrate the lair of the treacherous figure of The Rat. "My dear Watson," he began, his voice quivering with enthusiasm, "I propose that we assume the guises of lost American Mormons, our feigned disorientation and bewilderment serving as a Trojan horse that will allow us to penetrate the very heart of our quarry's domain."

Watson, however, appeared less than enamoured with this farcical proposition, his brow furrowed in consternation as he considered the merits of Holmes's plan. "Holmes," he retorted, "while I appreciate the ingenuity of your suggestion, I cannot help but feel that a more direct approach may be better suited to our present circumstances. Rather than adopting the absurd ruse of bewildered proselytizers, I propose that we burst into The Rat's lair, weapons threateningly brandished, and confront him with the full force of our righteous determination."

The ensuing debate between the two men grew increasingly heated, as Holmes clung tenaciously to his ludicrous plan while Watson advocated for a more direct, assertive course of action. The air was thick with the stilted and grandiloquent language that so often characterised their discussions, an unabating cascade of polysyllabic words and convoluted phrases that seemed to obfuscate the simplicity of their dilemma rather than illuminate it.

Holmes, ever the imbecilic enthusiast, appeared incapable of recognising the folly of his proposed course of action, his obstinate determination rendering him blind to the glaring impracticalities of his plan. Watson, however, remained resolute in his opposition, his voice firm and unwavering as he sought to dissuade his companion from embarking upon a course that would surely lead to their undoing.

Eventually, after much contentious disputation, Holmes acquiesced to Watson's wisdom, his pride begrudgingly yielding to the inescapable logic of his colleague's argument. "Very well, Watson," he murmured, his voice tinged with a hint of chagrin, "we shall proceed as you suggest, our weapons at the ready and our resolve unyielding. It is my fervent hope that this course of action will lead us to the swift apprehension of The Rat and the resolution of this most perplexing case."

With their strategy thus agreed upon, Holmes and Watson steeled themselves for the confrontation that lay ahead, their hearts emboldened by their shared determination to bring the villainous figure known as The Rat to justice. As they approached the lair, their steps resolute and purposeful, they could not help but feel a sense of trepidation, a frisson of anticipation that rippled through their very souls as they prepared to confront the orchestrator of the evil deeds that had so confounded and perplexed them.

As they drew nearer to the entrance of The Rat's lair, the gloom of the surrounding streets seemed to weigh heavily upon their shoulders, as if the very air was suffused with the taint of villainy that had led them to this desolate corner of London. Their hands tightened around the hilts of their weapons, the cold steel offering a semblance of reassurance amidst the oppressive darkness that enveloped them.

Holmes and Watson exchanged a final, meaningful glance, each man silently acknowledging the gravity of the moment and the potential dangers that lay ahead. With a curt nod, Watson signalled his readiness to proceed, and together they advanced upon the doorway that stood as the threshold between them and the shadowy figure whose machinations had so thoroughly ensnared them.

As they crossed that fateful threshold, their hearts pounding with a mixture of fear and determination, they steeled themselves for the confrontation that would determine the resolution of their most confounding and challenging case yet. Whether they would emerge victorious or succumb to the malevolent wiles of their quarry remained to be seen, but one thing was certain: they would not go down without a fight.

At long last, they arrived at the inner sanctum of The Rat, where they discovered the burglar engaged in the act of sorting through his ill-gotten gains from a long campaign of larceny. The man was a study in contrasts, his unassuming appearance belying the cunning and dexterity that had allowed him to perpetrate his abominable scheme undetected for so long. Holmes, unable to resist the temptation to engage in one final bout of theorising, whispered a convoluted explanation of The Rat's modus operandi to Watson, who listened with rapt attention.

Having sated their appetite for speculation, Holmes and Watson sprang into action, revolvers brandished, startling The Rat with their sudden appearance. The criminal, momentarily disoriented by the unexpected intrusion, attempted to flee, but his efforts were in vain. Holmes and Watson, their senses sharpened by the excitement of the chase, pursued their quarry with dogged determination, their voices raised in triumphant cries as they closed in on their prey.

Cornered and utterly devoid of alternatives, The Rat capitulated, his eyes brimming with an amalgamation of resignation and a palpable sense of defiance. Holmes, unable to quell the urge to boast, launched into an ostentatious soliloquy, elucidating the brilliance of his deductions and the inexorable nature of the burglar's apprehension. Watson, ever the steadfast compatriot, interjected with his own laudatory remarks, extolling the virtues of his associate's prodigious intellect and exceptional prowess.

During this bombastic display of self-congratulation, the capture of The Rat a mere inevitability, it became increasingly evident that the duo's vigilance had waned significantly. Indeed, the ebullient atmosphere appeared to provide the perfect opportunity for The Rat to exploit their momentary lapse in concentration. As I observed this precarious situation unfold from my unobtrusive vantage point, I understood that it was incumbent upon me to intervene and avert an imminent catastrophe.

In a swift and decisive move, I surreptitiously dislodged a sizeable flowerpot from a ledge above, causing it to plummet towards the cobblestone pavement below. The cacophonous crash proved sufficient to startle Holmes and Watson from their self-indulgent reverie, and they immediately refocused their attention on the apprehended criminal.

Simultaneously, the unexpected commotion had a profound effect on The Rat. His initial instinct was to exploit the pandemonium and attempt a desperate escape, but fate had other plans. In his haste to abscond, he unwittingly entangled himself in a cargo net that had been discarded nearby. The rope, as though possessed of a mind of its own, ensnared the malfeasant, rendering him utterly immobilised and conclusively thwarted in his efforts to evade capture.

Holmes, now fully cognisant of the gravity of the situation, immediately ceased his grandiose oration and sprang into action. He deftly secured the immobilised miscreant with the tangled net that had so fortuitously ensnared him, taking great care to ensure that the bindings were both secure and unyielding. Watson, not to be outdone, promptly aimed his trusty service revolver, effectively rendering him powerless and incapacitated.

With The Rat securely apprehended, Holmes and Watson exchanged a look of mingled relief and chagrin, as they belatedly realised the extent to which their overconfidence had nearly led to disaster. Nevertheless, they maintained a facade of stoicism and continued to expound upon their remarkable investigative abilities, choosing to attribute their success to their unerring intuition and keen observational skills, rather than the fortuitous intervention of an unseen ally.

As they escorted the defeated criminal to the waiting arms of the constabulary, I could not help but feel a twinge of satisfaction at having once again played a crucial role in the resolution of a perilous situation. Though Holmes and Watson remained blissfully ignorant of my involvement, I was content in the knowledge that, from the shadows, I had provided the crucial assistance necessary to ensure the triumph of justice over villainy.

However, the mastermind behind this case remained at large: Mr Marcel Merquin. I resolved to turn my attention to the matter of apprehending the cunning and duplicitous fiend, a rival inventor of considerable repute and cunning, whose machinations had long eluded the grasp of justice. Armed with my own formidable intellect and an unwavering commitment to the cause of righteousness, I embarked upon my pursuit of this elusive quarry with a steadfast determination that would, I hoped, ultimately lead to his capture and the restoration of balance to the fractured world of scientific endeavour.

As I traversed the imposing streets of our great metropolis, the moon casting shadows upon the cobbled thoroughfares, I reflected upon the various clues and whispers that had led me to this juncture, each disparate piece of information coalescing into a tapestry of intrigue and subterfuge. At length, I arrived at the seemingly innocuous abode of the malefactor, my heart quickening with anticipation as I steeled myself for the confrontation that I knew must surely lie ahead.

With utmost caution, I approached Merquin's dwelling, the creaking hinges of the front door providing a disquieting accompaniment to the palpable tension that now hung in the air like a malevolent miasma. Upon crossing the threshold, I was confronted with a sight that gave me pause; for the domicile, which I had expected to find teeming with evidence of Merquin's depraved activities, was entirely bereft of any such indications. Instead, the rooms lay empty and forlorn, as though they had been hastily abandoned by their erstwhile occupant. The walls, once adorned with the myriad accoutrements of scientific endeavour, now stared back at me in silent testimony to the void that had been left in their wake.

With a mounting sense of disquiet, I continued my exploration of the premises, my footsteps echoing through the desolate chambers as I endeavoured to discern some clue or trace of the fugitive inventor's whereabouts. Alas, my search proved fruitless, for it seemed that Merquin had taken great pains to cover his tracks, leaving behind naught but an eerie silence that seemed to mock my efforts.

The once-thriving laboratory, where I had anticipated discovering the secrets that lay at the heart of Merquin's schemes, now presented a tableau of emptiness and desolation, its erstwhile contents vanished as though spirited away by some opprobrious force. The realisation that my quarry had eluded me, perhaps anticipating a pursuit and making good his escape, filled me with a sense of frustration and chagrin that was difficult to shake.

As I stood amidst the disarray of Merquin's abandoned lair, contemplating the implications of my discovery, or rather, the lack thereof, I could not help but feel a sense of admiration for the cunning and guile of my adversary. For, in spite of my own considerable prowess, he had managed to slip through my grasp, leaving me to ponder the nature of the game that we now found ourselves engaged in, a game that was far from concluded.

And so, as I reluctantly took my leave of the desolate abode, my thoughts turned to the road that lay ahead, a road fraught with uncertainty and peril, yet one that I knew I must eventually traverse to bring Merquin's malevolent machinations to an end. For while the shadows that enveloped his flight seemed nigh impenetrable, I remained steadfast in my conviction that, with time and perseverance, I would ultimately pierce the veil of obfuscation that enshrouded his whereabouts. But, for now, I must accept that my quarry has absconded justice.

As I returned to the shadows whence I had emerged, my thoughts ever occupied with the elusive Merquin, I could not help but feel a sense of profound satisfaction in knowing that I had played a crucial role in the ongoing pursuit of justice. It was in this spirit that I continued to watch and wait, ever vigilant, ever prepared to step forth and lend my assistance to those who sought to uphold justice.

With the arrest of The Rat and the disappearance of Marcel Merquin, the curtain fell on yet another of Sherlock Holmes' legendary exploits, and the world continued to marvel at the seemingly supernatural abilities of the great detective. Little did they know that, hidden behind the scenes, a silent partner laboured in obscurity, orchestrating the events that would ultimately lead to the resolution of the case.

And so, with the case of the rival inventors brought to a satisfactory conclusion, I returned to my life of observation and contemplation. Holmes, meanwhile, continued to bask in the adulation of a grateful public, blissfully unaware of the guiding hand that had once again steered him towards the truth.

As I gazed out of my window, watching the comings and goings of the detective and his loyal companion, I could not help but smile at the farcical nature of it all. For, in the end, it was not the genius of Sherlock Holmes that held the key to the mysteries of the criminal world, but the unassuming figure who watched from his window, ever vigilant and ever ready to step in when the need arose.

Chapter 6: The Riddle of the Vanished Viscount

The first inklings of the new case arrived on a brisk and sunny morning, as the eager anticipation of the day's events filled the air. From my window, I observed the figure of a well-dressed, ruddy-faced gentleman making his way up the steps to the famed residence of Sherlock Holmes. He appeared to be in a state of some distress, his face flushed and his hands trembling as he clutched a crumpled note.

Upon being escorted into the sitting room by Billy, the gentleman introduced himself as Sir Petersen Moncreiffe, the uncle of Viscount Albert Montague, who had recently vanished under mysterious circumstances. The family, it seemed, was in a state of near panic, and Sir Petersen had been dispatched to enlist the aid of the illustrious detective in locating the missing nobleman.

Holmes, ever eager to display his prodigious powers of observation, leapt at the opportunity to dazzle his new client with a series of misguided deductions. "Ah, Sir Petersen," he declared, casting a cursory glance at the man's attire, "I deduce that you have travelled here from the countryside, most likely by means of steam. Furthermore, I perceive that your residence is situated near a large body of water, as evidenced by the faint scent of seaweed that lingers about your person. You like to read Dutch literature and have recently visited the opera".

Sir Petersen, clearly taken aback by Holmes's assertions, hesitated for a moment before replying, "I'm afraid you are quite mistaken, Mr Holmes. I reside in Belgravia, and I arrived here by means of a carriage. As for the scent you detected, I fear it must be a remnant of last night's dinner, which included a rather pungent seafood chowder. I cannot claim to have ever read any Dutch literature, as I am unable to speak the language, and I have a profound repulsion to the opera on account of my late mother having recently passed away during a performance of Puccini".

Holmes, undeterred by this rebuke, was dismissive and pressed Sir Petersen to continue with his account of the Viscount's disappearance. As the tale unfolded, it became apparent that young Montague had vanished without a trace, leaving behind a ransacked study and a series of cryptic notes, the meaning of which eluded even the most learned members of the family.

Throughout the interview, I listened intently from my vantage point, carefully noting each detail, and forming my own theories as to the nature of the mystery. Holmes, on the other hand, appeared to be more interested in the contents of his tobacco pouch than in the particulars of the case, his attention drifting in and out of the conversation with alarming frequency.

As the meeting drew to a close, Sir Petersen, clearly dubious of Holmes's abilities but desperate for any assistance he could find, implored the detective to take up the case. Holmes, sensing an opportunity for yet another dramatic display of his purported genius, eagerly accepted the challenge, promising, as usual, to leave no stone unturned in his search for the vanished Viscount.

With the client's departure, I knew that it would once again fall to me to delve into the heart of the mystery and to bring the truth to light. For, while Holmes might bumble his way through a thicket of red herrings and false leads, I was confident that my own keen powers of observation and deduction would prove more than equal to the task at hand.

And so, with a steely determination in my heart, I resolved to embark upon my own investigation, confident that the solution to the riddle of the vanished Viscount lay within my grasp. Little did I know that the labyrinthine twists and turns of the case would lead me down a path of deceit and treachery that would challenge even the most cunning of minds.

From my window, I listened as Holmes and Watson discussed the case, their countenance a mixture of excitement and self-satisfaction. Holmes, no doubt, was weaving another elaborate theory based on nothing more than his own misguided conjectures. I strained my ears to catch the details of their conversation.

"Now, Watson," Holmes proclaimed, his voice filled with a sense of grandiosity, "I have deduced that the true purpose of the Viscount's disappearance is, in fact, an attempt to destabilise the British Government. You see, the Viscount is a known associate of several influential politicians, and his sudden vanishing is sure to cause ripples of unease throughout the upper echelons of society."

Watson, ever the loyal sidekick, nodded his agreement, though it was evident that even he harboured some doubts as to the veracity of his friend's claims. "Indeed, Holmes, your deductions are nothing short of miraculous. However, I must confess, I fail to see how the ransacked study and cryptic notes fit into this grand scheme."

Holmes waved his pipe dismissively. "Elementary, my dear Watson. The study was ransacked to create the illusion of a struggle, while the notes were intentionally left behind to sow confusion and divert attention from the true purpose of the abduction."

Suppressing the urge to release a prolonged sigh of exasperation at the bewilderingly erroneous suppositions put forth by the esteemed Mr Holmes, I could not help but be cognisant of the fact that the reality of the matter was, in all likelihood, considerably more mundane. Resolute in my determination to uncover the veracity of the situation, I elected to embark upon my own discreet investigation, commencing with a hasty sojourn to the illustrious Montague family estate.

Having ascertained the location of the aforementioned domicile, I secured passage by hansom cab which conveyed me with alacrity across the verdant expanses of the English countryside. As the miles unfurled before me, I contemplated the forthcoming events, in which I would feign an acquaintance with a distant cousin of the Montague lineage, thereby procuring the requisite pretext for my intrusion upon their ancestral grounds.

Upon my arrival at the estate, I was struck by the grandiosity of its sylvan surroundings, which encompassed acres of meticulously manicured lawns, resplendent with vibrant flower beds and punctuated by stately topiary arrangements. The landscape was traversed by a labyrinthine network of gravel pathways, guiding the visitor through the picturesque gardens and towards the imposing edifice that was the Montague Manor House.

The manor itself was an honorary monument to architectural prowess, an amalgamation of Gothic and Tudor styles which loomed over the estate like a venerable sentinel. Its imposing façade was composed of intricately carved stonework, which appeared to defy the ravages of time as it retained the aura of a bygone era. The structure was crowned with an elaborate array of gables and turrets, their latticed windows casting an air of mystery upon the interior of the residence. Upon closer inspection, I noted the presence of ornate stone gargoyles, their grotesque visages leering down at me from their lofty perches, as if they were privy to some arcane secret which they were sworn to protect.

Bidding my driver to wait, I approached the entrance and was greeted by a formidable oak door, its surface etched with the patina of centuries and adorned with a massive brass knocker, fashioned in the likeness of a lion's head. The door creaked open to reveal a footman of impeccable bearing, who inquired as to my business upon the Montague estate. With an air of nonchalance, I proffered my fabricated tale of kinship with a distant cousin, and to my relief, the footman acquiesced, granting me entry into the hallowed halls of the manor.

Once inside, I found myself ensconced within an opulent vestibule, the grandeur of which was accentuated by the intricate plasterwork and gilded cornices which adorned the walls and ceilings. A magnificent crystal chandelier hung from above, casting a warm, inviting glow upon the polished marble floors and the luxurious Persian rugs which lay beneath my feet. The walls were adorned with a panoply of priceless artworks, each one a testament to the Montague family's refined sensibilities and exquisite taste.

As I proceeded to conduct my inquiries, I was conscious of the need for the utmost discretion, lest my true intentions be discerned by the ever-watchful eyes of the household staff. Thus, I endeavoured to navigate the quiet corridors and opulent chambers of the Montague Manor House with a carefully cultivated air of casual interest, all the while surreptitiously seeking out any clues which might illuminate the enigmatic circumstances surrounding the case at hand. Seeking solace by way of enquiring about the water closet, I closed in on the location of my investigation.

Upon entering the ransacked study, I was immediately struck by the disarray that reigned supreme within its once-stately confines. The room, adorned with lavish furnishings and sumptuous tapestries, bore testimony to the Viscount's predilection for opulence, yet the chaos that now prevailed bespoke of a heinous intrusion. As I scrutinised the scene, my eyes fell upon a veritable maelstrom of scattered papers and volumes, their presence suggestive of a desperate search for some item of immense import.

The study itself was a veritable treasure trove of curiosities and *objets d'art*, with richly carved mahogany bookcases lined with volumes of esoteric lore and leather-bound tomes, a testament to the Viscount's intellectual pursuits. The walls, festooned with exquisite works of art, bore witness to his refined taste and aesthetic sensibilities. An imposing desk of polished mahogany,

96

now marred by the upheaval, once served as the centrepiece of this sanctuary of erudition.

Amongst this chaotic tableau, I espied a missive from the Viscount's solicitor, its contents detailing a recent acquisition of valuable foreign stocks, an inheritance that had undoubtedly aroused the interest of unscrupulous parties. Further exploration of the study revealed a torn corner of an envelope, its partial address indicating a location in the less salubrious environs of the East End of London. This information, when considered in conjunction with the Viscount's well-documented proclivity for high-stakes gambling, led me to postulate that the crux of the case lay not in the realm of political subterfuge, but rather in the sordid domain of personal avarice.

It occurred to me, as I prepared to take my leave, that the malefactors were either unmindful of the considerable worth of the many exquisite art pieces in the chamber, or they were singularly intent on acquiring a particular object. A matter most intriguing, indeed.

Having obtained the clues I required, and under the pretence of returning from the water closet, I tendered my farewell to the attentive footman, effecting a precipitous departure and ensconcing myself within the confines of the patiently awaiting hansom cab.

Returning to my residence, I continued my research, delving into the underbelly of London's gambling scene in search of any connections to the Viscount or his mysterious inheritance. Meanwhile, I observed Holmes as he embarked on a wild goose chase, pursuing various politicians and government officials in a vain attempt to uncover their non-existent involvement in the case.

Through assiduous inquiries and the employment of keen observation, I embarked upon the onerous task of discerning the whereabouts of the missing Viscount. My enquiries led me to engage in discreet conversations with an assortment of individuals, ranging from hansom cab drivers to loquacious street vendors, each contributing a fragment of information that, when assembled, began to form a coherent picture of the Viscount's activities.

As my enquiries bore fruit, it became increasingly evident that the Viscount's movements had drawn him into the seedy underbelly of London's East End, where he had become ensnared by a notorious gambling den known to harbour all manner of unscrupulous characters. Recognising the need for a suitable disguise to infiltrate this den of iniquity, I donned the attire of a well-to-do patron, adorning myself with a carefully chosen assortment of garments designed to project an air of affluence whilst avoiding undue attention. Thus disguised, I ventured forth into the maw of the gambling establishment, hoping to glean further information about the Viscount's unfortunate predicament.

Upon entering the dimly lit, smoke-filled establishment, the pungent odour of tobacco and the cacophony of raised voices assaulted my senses. I cautiously navigated the network of gaming tables, observing the desperate faces of patrons as they wagered their fortunes on games of chance. As I surreptitiously listened in on conversations between the patrons of this sordid establishment, I began to piece together the events that had led to the Viscount's current plight.

It transpired that the Viscount, a novice in the perilous world of gambling, had been expertly ensnared by a ruthless gang of cardsharps who preyed upon the unwary and inexperienced. These cunning miscreants had lured the unsuspecting Viscount into their clutches with promises of excitement and the prospect of easy winnings. Little did the Viscount know that he had, in fact, been led like a lamb to the slaughter, the cardsharps' true intent being to swindle him out of his newly acquired fortune.

The machinations of these unscrupulous villains had been executed with great subtlety and skill, as they plied the Viscount with alcohol and the attention of *demi-mondaines*, clouding his judgement and impairing his ability to perceive the true nature of the high-stakes game he had become embroiled in. As the stakes grew ever higher, the Viscount found himself ensnared in a web of deceit, unable to extricate himself from the clutches of his merciless captors, who stood poised to relieve him of his entire fortune.

Incapable of settling the accumulating debts at that precise juncture, the Viscount had shared information with his captors regarding a compendium of stock certificates stored safely within the sanctum of his study. This prompted the disarray and violation of said chamber, and shredded light upon the criminal activities that had transpired therein.

Thus, the full extent of the Viscount's plight had been laid bare before me, and I became acutely aware of the urgency of the situation. It was imperative that I take swift action to rescue the hapless Viscount from his captors and return him to the safety of his family, lest he be forever lost in the dark and treacherous underworld that had claimed so many unfortunate souls before him. With this revelation in hand, I knew it was time to once again guide the hapless Holmes to the truth. Crafting an anonymous letter containing carefully chosen hints and clues, I posted it through the letterbox at 221B Baker Street, hoping that it would be enough to steer the great detective toward the true solution to the case.

As I returned to my position at the window, I could not help but shake my head at Holmes' dire approach in this case. For, while the bumbling Holmes continued to grasp at the flimsiest of straws, it was I, the unassuming Horatio Ollerenthorpe, who had once again unravelled the tangled threads of the mystery and brought the truth to light.

Later, I watched from my window as Holmes and Watson returned from their foray into the East End gambling den, both looking rather worse for wear. Their clothes were dishevelled, and Holmes sported a rather impressive black eye, evidence of a scuffle that had clearly not gone in his favour.

As they entered their sitting room, I strained to catch the details of their conversation. Holmes, trying to maintain an air of nonchalance, recounted the events of their visit. "Watson, I must admit that the situation at the gambling den took an unexpected turn. I attempted to confront the cardsharps using my extensive knowledge of bartitsu, but alas, it seems they were somewhat more proficient in the pugilistic arts than I had anticipated."

Watson looked both concerned and bemused. "Well, Holmes, at least we have established the Viscount's whereabouts and the company he is keeping. But how do we proceed now? We cannot simply barge into the gambling den again and extract him by force."

"That, my dear Watson, is a three-pipe problem. Please go about your business whilst I sit and smoke," and Holmes retreated into a *brown study*.

Holmes was clearly out of his depth in this situation. It was then that I decided to intervene once more, providing the beleaguered detective with a plan to ensnare the cardsharps and rescue the Viscount.

Disguised as a messenger boy, I hurried to Baker Street and slipped a note into the hands of Billy the page. The note, written in the style of a mysterious informant, detailed a proposal to host a high-stakes card game at the prestigious Turf Club in Piccadilly, wagering the Viscount's freedom against a considerable sum of £1,000 in gold. The cardsharps, unable to resist the lure of such an enticing offer, would surely attend, providing Holmes with the opportunity to apprehend them and rescue the Viscount.

Holmes, upon reading the note, was initially sceptical but soon became enamoured with the idea. "Watson, this may be the very opportunity we need to bring this sordid affair to a close. We shall prepare for this game at the Turf Club and ensure that justice is served."

In the hallowed halls of the Turf Club, an institution renowned for its devotion to high-stakes gambling, the stage was set for an extraordinary confrontation that would not only bring the cardsharps to justice but also provide a fitting conclusion to the series of cases that had vexed Holmes and Watson for so many months. The ruse was simple: Holmes and Watson, disguising themselves as wealthy gentlemen with a penchant for gambling, would lure the cardsharps into a trap, with the able assistance of the club's security and several plain-clothes police officers. I, a casual observer in the guise of a retired, mutton-chopped Member of Parliament.

The plan, however, would require both skill and subtlety, qualities which, as I had observed on numerous occasions, were not always present in the detective's repertoire. Nevertheless, the game, as Holmes is always eager to announce, was afoot!

The evening began with a palpable sense of tension, as Holmes and Watson took their places at the gaming table. Despite the black eye he had acquired in their previous encounter, Holmes endeavoured to maintain an air of indifference, though his efforts were somewhat marred by his apparent inability to suppress the occasional wince of pain. Watson, for his part, appeared to be equally ill at ease, his gaze darting nervously about the room as he struggled to maintain the facade of a carefree gambler.

As the card game commenced, it quickly became apparent that subtlety was not to be the order of the evening. Holmes, in an attempt to convey an air of insouciance, engaged in a series of increasingly ludicrous bluffs, wagering exorbitant sums on the flimsiest of hands. The cardsharps, sensing that their prey was within their grasp, eagerly took the bait, raising the stakes to dizzying heights.

The atmosphere in the room grew ever more charged, as the other players looked on in a mixture of bemusement and disbelief. I, from my vantage point near the bar, could scarcely contain my amusement at the spectacle unfolding before me. Holmes' performance was, in a word, farcical, a fact that seemed to escape neither the cardsharps nor the plain-clothes police officers who looked on with barely concealed consternation.

The denouement of this grand charade came as a most unexpected turn of events. In a twist of fate that could only be described as serendipitous, Holmes, in the final hand of the game, found himself in possession of four aces, a hand that, by any standard, was nigh unbeatable. His eyes widened in astonishment, the great detective could scarcely believe his good fortune, and with a flourish that bordered on the melodramatic, he revealed his cards to the stunned assembly.

The cardsharps, realising that their nefarious scheme was coming undone, reacted with predictable violence. Amidst the dimly lit and smoke-filled room of the Turf Club, the air grew thick with tension as the malefactors brandished their concealed weapons, their countenances twisted into faces of unbridled fury.

Holmes, ever the optimistic, yelled "Get the blighters!" However, the criminals were first to move, with nary a moment's hesitation. They launched themselves at Holmes and Watson, intent on exacting a brutal retribution for their unmasking. The cacophony of discordant shouts and the thunderous collision of bodies echoed throughout the chamber, as the two adversaries engaged in a fierce and desperate struggle for supremacy.

Holmes, unwittingly in the fray, sought to parry the blows that rained down upon him, his limbs darting this way and that in an attempt to evade the relentless assault. However, ever overconfident in his skills in the art of self-defence, he succumbed to the onslaught, and a particularly savage blow connected with his countenance, causing his other eye to blacken and swell with alarming rapidity.

Watson, ever the loyal companion, leapt into the fray with the valour of a seasoned warrior, his fists striking with neither precision nor force. In the heat of the mêlée, the combatants exchanged heated invectives, their voices raised in a chorus of anger and defiance that resonated throughout the room, adding to the sense of chaos that had swiftly enveloped the once convivial gathering.

In response to the escalating violence, having witnessed enough of our heroes' ineptitude, the plain-clothes officers who had accompanied Holmes and Watson eventually sprang into action, their well-honed instincts and *lignum vitae* truncheons guiding them as they moved to subdue the miscreants with considerable efficiency. Employing the necessary force required to quell the burgeoning tumult, they grappled with the assailants, their steely determination matched only by their unwavering commitment to the cause of justice.

As the conflict raged, the other patrons of the Turf Club, their faces etched with terror, made haste to flee the scene, abandoning their once convivial pursuits in favour of self-preservation. The once bustling room, filled with laughter and the clink of glassware, now echoed with the tumultuous sounds of strife and pandemonium, as furniture toppled, and glass shattered underfoot. At some point in the fray, one lanky cardsharp with a cheroot hanging from the side of his mouth, was propelled across the room beside me. As he turned around to re-join the battle, barely recognising the presence of an aged MP, I took the opportunity to incapacitate him with a wooden stool, hitting him squarely on the noggin.

However, amidst the chaos, a small cadre of stalwart observers remained, their gazes riveted upon the unfolding spectacle. Their expressions varied from curiosity to thinly veiled amusement, as they watched the events unfold with a mixture of fascination and trepidation. Some among them whispered hurried conjectures as to the identities of the combatants, while others simply observed in stoic silence, their faces betraying no hint of emotion.

In the midst of this extraordinary drama, the air was thick with the acrid scent of smoke and the mingled odours of spilled spirits and sweat, as the combatants fought with a ferocity born of desperation and the immutable desire to emerge victorious. As the final act of this vociferous affair played out before them, the onlookers could not help but be enthralled by the spectacle, for it was a scene rarely witnessed within the oak-panelled walls of the Turf Club, and one which would undoubtedly be recounted with breathless excitement for many years to come.

In the end, the cardsharps were led away in handcuffs, their enterprise brought to an ignominious end. Holmes, still reeling from the unlikely confluence of events that had culminated in his victory, attempted to regain his composure, though his efforts were somewhat hampered by the effects of two black eyes and the raucous laughter of his erstwhile accomplices.

As the dust settled and the last echoes of mirth faded from the walls of the Turf Club, Holmes and Watson exchanged glances, their expressions a mixture of relief and disbelief. The great detective, despite his numerous missteps and a conspicuous lack of subtlety, had somehow managed to emerge victorious, his reputation as the scourge of London's criminal underworld remaining intact. Watson, loyal friend to the end, patted Holmes on the back, a gesture that seemed to simultaneously convey both admiration and bemusement.

In the quiet aftermath of the rumbustious evening, the participants in this most peculiar of dramas began to disperse, leaving the once-peaceful club in a state of disarray. The plain-clothes officers, their task complete, filed out of the room, their faces creased with smirks and stifled laughter. The security personnel, having borne witness to a scene unlike any they had previously encountered, exchanged bemused glances, no doubt wondering what other surprises the future might hold.

As for myself, I remained in the shadows, my role in the proceedings known to none but me. It had been my careful deductions and timely interventions that had led to the downfall of the criminal masterminds behind the web of intrigues that had ensnared the city. Yet I harboured no desire for recognition or glory; my sole concern was the pursuit of justice, and the knowledge that I had played my part in its service was reward enough.

As Holmes and Watson departed the Turf Club, their heads held high and their spirits buoyed by their improbable victory, I could not help but smile. In spite of his many foibles and the sometimes farcical nature of his methods, Sherlock Holmes remained a force to be reckoned with, his indomitable spirit and unerring dedication to his craft an inspiration to all who knew him. And though I remained in the shadows, forever observing and guiding from a distance, I took solace in the knowledge that, together, we had brought justice to those who sought to evade its grasp, and restored order to the chaos that had threatened to engulf the city.

Incarcerated, the gang of cardsharps were motivated by the force of truncheons to reveal the location of the bound and gagged Viscount, who was emancipated with great relief and a modicum of shame, back into the bosom of his family. A note of gratitude followed, from the grateful yet surprised Sir Petersen Moncreiffe.

Thus, with the final chapter of this most extraordinary case drawing to a close, I retreated once more to the sanctuary of my lodgings, my thoughts already turning to the next great adventure that awaited us. For in the ever-shifting landscape of

Victorian London, there was always another mystery to be solved, another puzzle to be unravelled, and another villain to be vanquished. And in the pursuit of these lofty goals, I knew that I would never be alone, for the great Sherlock Holmes, imbecile though he might be, would always be there, a constant presence in the shadows, a reminder that justice, no matter how elusive, would always prevail.

As for me, Horatio Ollerenthorpe, I observed the unfolding events from the shadows, taking quiet satisfaction in the knowledge that I had played a significant role in resolving the case. For, in the end, it was not the bumbling detective's farcical antics that had brought about the solution, but rather the unseen hand of a humble neighbour who had guided him, step by step, toward the truth.

Chapter 6: The Disappearance of Mycroft Holmes

From my window, I observed as Sherlock Holmes and Dr Watson prepared to leave their sitting room, bound for the Diogenes Club. Holmes was visibly concerned, the furrows in his brow betraying his worry. "Watson," he declared, "we must make haste. I have received word that my brother Mycroft has not been seen at the club for several days. This is most unusual, and I fear that some sinister plot may be afoot."

As they set off down Baker Street, I could not help but chuckle at the thought of the ever-incompetent Holmes attempting to unravel a conspiracy involving his own brother. The farcical nature of his previous cases had provided me with no end of amusement, and I had little doubt that this new adventure would prove just as entertaining. As was my way, I followed the duo and maintained my anonymity from the shadows, carefully disguised as a well-groomed gentleman.

Upon their arrival at the Diogenes Club, Holmes and Watson were greeted by a flustered club secretary, who informed them that Mycroft had indeed vanished without a trace. Holmes, in his typical impetuous manner, immediately leaped to the conclusion that his brother's disappearance was part of a plot to bring down the British government.

"My dear sir," Holmes exclaimed to the club secretary, "it is evident that we are dealing with a matter of national security! My brother is an indispensable asset to our government, and his sudden absence can only mean that he has been abducted by evil forces seeking to destabilise our great nation!"

The club secretary, clearly nonplussed by Holmes's dramatics, attempted to placate the agitated detective. "Mr Holmes, while it is true that your brother's disappearance is most irregular, I would caution against jumping to such alarming conclusions. There may be a simpler explanation for his absence."

Holmes, however, would not be swayed. "Nonsense!" he retorted. "There is no time to waste on idle speculation. Watson and I must begin our investigation at once and track down the fiends responsible for my brother's abduction!"

The pair left the Diogenes Club in haste, their coats billowing behind them like the sails of a ship caught in a tempest. Upon reaching Baker Street, they wasted not a moment in the preparation of their disguises. Holmes, eccentric as expected, opted for the appearance of a dishevelled street vendor, complete with tattered garments and a grime-streaked visage. Watson, on the other hand, attempted to embody the demeanour of a respectable gentleman of leisure, though his attire and bearing were more reminiscent of a comically out-of-place country squire than a man of refined taste.

As I observed their ludicrous metamorphoses from the vantage point of my concealed window, I could not help but feel a pang of concern for their endeavours. Nonetheless, I resolved to shadow their movements and, donning the guise of a hansom cab driver, followed them to the heart of Whitehall.

The bustling thoroughfare teemed with a panoply of civil servants and officials, each absorbed in their own affairs and wholly oblivious to the ludicrous pair that had infiltrated their ranks. Despite their outlandish appearances, Holmes and Watson managed, through sheer force of will, to strike up conversations with several unsuspecting individuals.

Holmes, adopting an affected cockney accent that would have made a true denizen of the East End cringe, plied his unwitting interlocutors with a series of inane questions regarding Mycroft's whereabouts. "Oi, guv'nor," he would begin, his voice strained with the effort of maintaining the unconvincing dialect, "I 'eard tell of a bloke by the name of Mycroft, a right clever cove, 'e is. D'ya 'appen to know where I might find 'im?"

Watson, for his part, fared little better in his attempts to elicit information. His affected air of nonchalance did little to mask his anxiety, and his queries were often met with puzzled stares and, on one occasion, a curt dismissal from a particularly haughty undersecretary.

Unbeknownst to them, I maintained a watchful eye from a position within my hansom cab, ready to intervene should their bumbling efforts at subterfuge result in calamity. As they approached my vehicle, I overheard their breathless conversation, each attempting to outdo the other in recounting the details of their respective escapades.

"By Jove, Holmes!" Watson exclaimed, his eyes alight with excitement. "I have never engaged in such a daring scheme! I must say, the information we have gleaned today will undoubtedly prove invaluable in locating our dear friend Mycroft."

Holmes, not to be outdone, nodded sagely in agreement. "Elementary, my dear Watson," he replied, his voice still tinged with the remnants of his atrocious accent. "The clues we have unearthed shall doubtlessly illuminate the murky depths of this perplexing enigma."

In truth, their efforts had yielded little more than a smattering of inconsequential titbits, yet their boundless enthusiasm was not to be dampened. As they climbed into my cab, I could not help but marvel at their unshakeable determination.

With a crack of the reins, and an explosive fart from the old nag in front, I set our course for Baker Street, my heart swelling with a curious mixture of trepidation and anticipation. For, despite their bumbling demeanour and near-constant propensity for farce, I knew that there was something indefinable about the duo of Holmes and Watson, a spark of brilliance that, when ignited, could set the world ablaze. And as we traversed the cobbled streets of London, I could not help but feel that I was an integral part of their grand adventure, even if my presence remained unbeknownst to them.

Upon our return to Baker Street, the pair alighted my cab and retreated to their lodgings, their minds ablaze with plans and stratagems for the next stage of their investigation. Ensconced in the comfort of their familiar surroundings, after tea and generous slices of cake provided by Mrs Hudson, they began to piece together the scant information they had gathered, their conversation punctuated by bouts of laughter and the occasional exclamation of triumph.

"Clearly, Watson," Holmes declared, his voice dripping with self-satisfaction, "our foray into the heart of the bureaucratic leviathan has yielded results most fortuitous. By my estimation, we are but a hair's breadth away from unearthing the truth behind Mycroft's mysterious disappearance."

Watson, ever the faithful companion, nodded in enthusiastic agreement. "Indeed, Holmes," he concurred, "I daresay our combined efforts shall prove more than equal to the task at hand. Soon, the truth shall be laid bare, and the veil of secrecy that has shrouded this affair shall be lifted."

As I listened to their impassioned discourse from my vantage point, I could not help but feel a twinge of admiration for their indomitable spirit. Despite the myriad obstacles that had been placed before them, and indeed created by them, they remained steadfast in their pursuit of truth and justice.

Meanwhile, I employed my own methods to investigate Mycroft's disappearance. Using my connections within London's criminal underworld, I managed to uncover several intriguing pieces of information. While Holmes's wild theories about a plot to bring down the government appeared to be unfounded, it seemed that

Mycroft had indeed become entangled in some dangerous business.

My investigations had led me to a secretive society known as The Elysium Brotherhood, an illicit organisation that wielded considerable influence within the city's criminal underworld. As I began my inquiries into the shadowy world of The Elysium Brotherhood, I found myself navigating a labyrinth of whispers and half-truths, encountering a host of disreputable characters who seemed to materialise out of the very ether. These denizens of London's seedy underbelly, bound by a code of silence, were reticent to divulge any information regarding the impenetrable organisation.

Undeterred, I endeavoured to lift the veil of secrecy that shrouded the Brotherhood, adopting a series of guises and false identities to insinuate myself further into the criminal underworld. My efforts eventually bore fruit, and I found myself in possession of a veritable treasure trove of intelligence concerning the Brotherhood's activities.

It transpired that the organisation was responsible for a plethora of criminal enterprises, their tentacles of influence extending into a wide variety of criminal endeavours. Their devilry had been orchestrated with such precision and cunning that they had hitherto remained undetected by the authorities, their very existence the stuff of whispered legend.

My inquiries led me to a series of secret meetings, held in the dead of night in the dank and fetid back alleys of London's East End. Here, amidst the choking fog and the ever-present stench of decay, I encountered the sinister agents of the Brotherhood, their faces shrouded in shadow, their voices little more than guttural whispers.

Through careful observation and painstaking detective work, I was able to piece together a jigsaw of information, each fragment providing me with greater insight into the Brotherhood's inner workings. I discovered that the organisation was led by a mysterious figure; a man - or woman - whose true identity remained shrouded in mystery.

It was this enigmatic figure who had ensnared Mycroft in their web of intrigue, using him as a pawn in their insidious game. I knew that I had little time to waste if I was to extricate the elder Holmes from the clutches of the Brotherhood, and so I set about devising a plan to infiltrate their inner sanctum.

In my tireless pursuit of this Brotherhood and their hidden activities, I found myself exceedingly grateful for the assistance rendered by my steadfast cadre of trusted informants, each endowed with an array of skills and aptitudes uniquely suited to the task at hand. Through the combined efforts of these intrepid allies, we embarked upon an arduous and labyrinthine journey into the shadowy underbelly of London society, unearthing long-buried secrets and exposing the malevolent forces that lurked behind the facade of respectability and propriety.

My first ally, the redoubtable Mr Stephen Galbraith, proved indispensable in our quest to penetrate the veil of secrecy that shrouded the Brotherhood's activities. A former member of the constabulary, Mr Galbraith had long since traded in his truncheon and uniform for the more clandestine pursuits of a private investigator, and his knowledge of the inner workings of London's criminal underworld proved most enlightening. Through a series of cautiously arranged meetings in the darkest recesses of the city's myriad public houses and opium dens, Mr Galbraith was able to elicit tantalising snippets of information from his many contacts, slowly but surely weaving together a tapestry of evidence that pointed inexorably towards the Brotherhood's hidden lair.

My next collaborator, Miss Arabella McDonald, brought to bear her formidable talents as a skilled linguist and codebreaker, her keen intellect and analytical prowess providing the means to decipher the cryptic missives and encoded communiques that we had thus far managed to intercept. Working tirelessly into the small hours of the night, Miss McDonald meticulously unravelled the tangled skein of riddles, gradually unearthing the secrets that lay at the very heart of the Brotherhood's labyrinthine organisation.

Meanwhile, the inimitable Mr Cornelius Durant, a gentleman of considerable charm and élan, utilised his considerable social connections and ingratiating manner to insinuate himself into the confidence of the Brotherhood's more gullible and impressionable members. Over the course of many a soiree and salon, Mr Durant was able to glean vital information regarding the inner workings and hierarchy of the shadowy cabal, providing us with an invaluable insight into the activities of our elusive quarry.

As our investigation proceeded apace, our final ally, the resourceful and enigmatic Mrs Cassandra O'Reilly, lent her prodigious talents as a master of disguise and subterfuge to our cause. Through her uncanny ability to blend seamlessly into her surroundings, Mrs O'Reilly was able to infiltrate the Brotherhood's network of spies and informants, surreptitiously gathering crucial intelligence regarding their movements and operations.

With the combined efforts of these stalwart companions, I meticulously pieced together the myriad fragments of information and evidence that we had amassed, ultimately discerning a discernible pattern amidst the chaos and obfuscation. Through our painstaking research and dogged determination, we were at last able to ascertain the precise location of the Brotherhood's secret sanctum, a subterranean lair cunningly concealed beneath the unassuming exterior of a humble tobacconist's shop in the heart of Whitechapel. The revelation of this hitherto unsuspected bastion of villainy marked a significant turning point in my investigation, bringing me one step closer to unmasking the mastermind behind the Brotherhood's malevolent schemes.

With this invaluable information to hand, I formulated a daring plan to infiltrate the Brotherhood's stronghold and rescue Mycroft from their clutches, with the witless assistance of Sherlock Holmes.

The following day, with the bustling streets of London awash in the golden glow of morning sunlight, I set my plan in motion. Clad in a convincing disguise as a street urchin, I made my way to the entrance of 221B Baker Street, where I would surreptitiously leave a message for Holmes and Watson, guiding them towards the truth of Mycroft's disappearance.

My message, hastily scrawled on a scrap of parchment, provided Holmes and Watson with the name and location of their quarry. As I slipped the note beneath the door of Holmes's residence, I could only hope that it would be enough to set them on the right path, and that they would extricate themselves from their misguided theories and wild conjecture.

Meanwhile, Holmes and Watson, recovering from another exhausting day of fruitless investigation in Whitehall, were enjoying a hearty breakfast of sausages and bacon within the confines of their Baker Street lodgings. Holmes, still determined to unravel the mystery of his brother's disappearance, eagerly awaited the arrival of the morning's post, hoping for some vital clue or lead to present itself.

"Ah, Watson," Holmes declared as he tore open an envelope, "the post has arrived! Perhaps it contains some vital piece of information that will aid us in our search for Mycroft!"

On cue, Holmes's attention was soon drawn to the note I had left beneath their door. Eagerly snatching it up, he read aloud its contents, his voice betraying a mixture of excitement and disbelief.

"'Phineas T. Wraith, The Elysium Brotherhood, Whitechapel,'" he recited, his eyes wide with amazement. "Watson, could it be that this message holds the key to Mycroft's disappearance?"

Watson, ever the pragmatist, responded cautiously. "Well, Holmes, it's certainly an intriguing lead. But we must be careful not to jump to conclusions. We know little of this Elysium Brotherhood, and even less about this Phineas T. Wraith."

Undeterred by his friend's caution, I could hear Holmes spring to his feet, his eyes no doubt alight with enthusiasm and his lap smeared with bacon grease. "Nonsense, Watson! This is precisely the breakthrough we've been waiting for! We must make haste to Whitechapel and confront this mysterious Wraith at once!"

And so, with renewed vigour, Holmes and Watson embarked upon the next stage of their investigation, unwittingly guided by the hidden hand of their secretive neighbour, Horatio Ollerenthorpe. As they made their way to the heart of Whitechapel with I, stealthily in tow, the tangled web of mystery surrounding Mycroft's disappearance began to unravel, revealing the sordid underbelly of London's criminal world, and the dangerous underworld of The Elysium Brotherhood.

Disguised as a member of the clergy, I strolled nonchalantly through the grimy streets of Whitechapel, keeping a close eye on Holmes and Watson as they approached the tobacconist's shop. Though I had provided them with a clear lead, Holmes, in his usual imbecilic manner, seemed far more preoccupied with the shop's selection of shag tobacco than the task at hand.

Eventually, Holmes approached the shop proprietor with an air of feigned casualness, engaging him in conversation while attempting to employ his deductive reasoning. "Ah, good sir," Holmes began, "I deduce from the calluses on your hands and the lingering scent of the sea that you are, in fact, a retired sailor, are you not?"

The proprietor raised an eyebrow, clearly bemused by Holmes's assertion. "Not in the slightest, sir. I've lived in nearby Wapping my entire life and have never set foot on a ship. In fact, merely thinking about taking to the water on a boat gives my stomach good reason to somersault".

As Holmes continued to flounder in his attempts to extract information from the shopkeeper, I took advantage of the distraction to slip around to the rear of the establishment. There, hidden beneath a trapdoor obscured by a pile of crates, I discovered the entrance to the lair of Phineas T. Wraith and his Elysium Brotherhood cohorts.

Carefully, I made my way down the dark, dank staircase, my ears attuned to the faint sounds of conversation echoing from below. As I reached the bottom, I caught sight of Wraith himself, a tall, sinister figure clad in a dark cloak, surrounded by his criminal associates.

Quickly devising a plan, I knocked over an oil lantern hanging nearby, causing the flames to spread rapidly across the floor. The resulting commotion and chaos forced Wraith and his henchmen to flee their hideout, providing the perfect opportunity for Holmes and Watson to intercept them.

Holmes, finally alerted to the true nature of the situation, burst through the rear door of the tobacconist's shop just in time to see Wraith and his men emerge from the hidden lair. With an uncharacteristic display of agility, Holmes and Watson gave chase, pursuing the fleeing criminals through the labyrinthine streets of Whitechapel.

As the chaotic chase unfolded, I maintained a discreet distance, ready to intervene if necessary. The pursuit south through Shadwell eventually led us to the banks of the Thames, where

Wraith began to take pot-shots at his pursuers. The customary click of an empty revolver prompted him to make a desperate attempt to double-back and escape, and so began to run precariously along the Thames wall in my direction.

Holmes, now displaying a characteristic lack of physical prowess, struggled to keep up with the nimble criminal. Sensing that the situation called for a more subtle approach, I poised myself as Wraith drew closer, my walking staff at the ready.

Wraith reached my position without displaying concern, observing merely a hunched man of the cloth. However, his disregard offered me the opportunity to take action. I deftly extended my staff, tripping Wraith as he attempted to make a daring leap across a gap onto a wooden scaffold. Wraith's body twisted in mid-air, and with a sickening crunch, he met his untimely end upon the unforgiving rocks below. I quickly melted into a crowd of curious onlookers.

Not wasting any time, Holmes turned back towards the tobacconist shop. On returning to the lair, Holmes rescued his bound and gagged brother who quickly recovered his composition, and air of authority. Dusting himself off, Mycroft regaled the story of his capture and subsequent incarceration beneath the tobacconists. Only half paying attention, Holmes took an unwavering interest in the diverse crates of shag tobacco, pilfering a sufficient enough bolus to fill the Persian slipper waiting for him back in Baker Street.

With the mastermind behind The Elysium Brotherhood defeated, the case of Mycroft's disappearance could finally be laid to rest. And once again, it was the unseen efforts of Horatio Ollerenthorpe, rather than the deranged antics of Sherlock Holmes, that had brought a dangerous criminal to justice.

Holmes and Watson returned to Baker Street, their heads held high, basking in the illusion of yet another triumphant victory.

They strode into 221B with the air of conquering heroes, unaware of the true orchestrator of their success. I listened to them from the shadows of my own abode, knowing that their pride was undeserved, but taking a certain satisfaction in having once again played a vital role in the apprehension of a dangerous criminal.

As they settled into the familiar surroundings of their sitting room, Holmes regaled Watson with a wildly inaccurate and exaggerated account of their Whitechapel adventure. He embellished every detail, painting himself as the fearless and brilliant mastermind who had single-handedly brought down the Elysium Brotherhood.

Watson, ever the faithful companion, hung on to every word, scribbling away in his notebook, eager to immortalise their latest escapade for posterity and personal profit. He listened with rapt attention as Holmes described how his supposed skills of deduction and keen intuition had led them to the heart of Wraith's lair, obviously omitting any mention of my covert assistance.

As the evening wore on, the pair continued to revel in their supposed success, toasting each other with glasses of fine sherry and puffing away on their pipes stuffed with purloined tobacco. They remained blissfully ignorant of the true extent of their folly, content to bask in the glory that they believed was rightfully theirs.

From the seclusion of my own home, I listened to the scene unfold with a mixture of amusement and resignation. Though I knew that the credit for solving the case truly belonged to me, I accepted my role as the unsung hero, the unseen guardian who kept the streets of London safe from the shadows.

For now, the city could rest easy, knowing that Phineas T. Wraith and his Elysium Brotherhood had been vanquished. But as long as Sherlock Holmes continued to blunder his way through investigations, I, Horatio Ollerenthorpe, would remain ever vigilant, ready to step in and set things right when the bumbling detective inevitably stumbled off course.

Chapter 7: The Duchess's Dilemma

One fine morning, as I peered out from behind the curtains of my study window, I observed a new client arriving at 221B Baker Street. A most striking woman, dressed in the height of fashion, her plumage a veritable symphony of silk and lace. Her presence exuded an air of refinement and elegance that was unmistakable, and it was quite clear that this was a lady of some consequence. Her gaze, however, betrayed a hint of unease, suggesting that her visit to the great detective was of a most urgent nature.

As the lady swept into the sitting room, I strained to catch the conversation that ensued. Holmes, in his characteristic manner, attempted to deduce the particulars of the client's identity and her reason for seeking his aid.

"Ah, madam," he proclaimed with an air of self-assurance, "I perceive that you have recently travelled from the north, most likely Yorkshire, judging by the hue of the remnants of mud upon your boots. Furthermore, I deduce that you have come by way of hansom cab, as evidenced by the slight fraying on the hem of your fine gown. Your gloves suggest that you keep dogs; a Scottish terrier I am confident in deducing."

The lady, a touch of incredulity in her voice, replied, "Mr Holmes, I must confess that your deductions are entirely mistaken. I have, in fact, come from the south, from Sussex in fact. My husband and I have a country estate there. As for my mode of transportation, I arrived in my own private carriage, not a hansom cab. As for my gloves, I have recently been afflicted with mild hair loss, and I would be grateful if you were not to mention it again."

Holmes, flustered by his erroneous conclusions, attempted to recover by diverting the conversation to the matter at hand. "My apologies, madam. Please do tell me how I may be of service to you. Whilst you do, let me get us some tea." As it was Billy's day off, Holmes shouted for the assistance of Mrs Hudson, who entered the room and curtsied towards the lady, whom she clearly recognised.

The lady, now identified as the Duchess of Wexford, began to recount her tale. It seemed that a priceless family heirloom, a necklace featuring the magnificent 'MacGuffin Diamond', had gone missing from her family residence, and she was desperate to recover it before an important society event later that month. The local constabulary had been unable to locate the missing jewels, and in her desperation, she had turned to Sherlock Holmes for assistance.

As I listened to the Duchess's tale, I could not help but chuckle at the farcical nature of Holmes's earlier deductions. Though he fancied himself a master of observation and logic, it seemed that his skills were more in the realm of pure fantasy than reality. I resolved to once again step in and guide the hapless detective towards the truth, using my keen intellect and subtle influence to ensure that justice was served, and the Duchess's precious heirloom was returned to its rightful owner.

As I listened intently to the conversation through the open window, I could scarcely believe the outlandish theory that Holmes was expounding upon with great gusto. He was adamant that the theft of the MacGuffin Diamond was but a small part of a nefarious scheme to finance a group of dangerous anarchists, intent on destabilising the very foundations of the British Empire.

"My dear Duchess," Holmes declared, "I have reason to believe that your missing heirloom is, in fact, at the centre of a vast conspiracy, the likes of which threatens the very existence of our great nation. I must embark on this case at once, for the fate of the empire hangs in the balance!"

With a mix of concern and confusion, the Duchess agreed to allow Holmes to pursue his peculiar line of inquiry. She provided him with the necessary information regarding her estate, and within the hour, Holmes and his faithful companion, Dr Watson, were *en route* to Sussex, Watson with his service revolver stowed safely in his breast pocket.

I, on the other hand, had my doubts regarding Holmes's outlandish theory. It seemed far more likely that the motive behind the theft was of a far more mundane nature. I decided to conduct my own investigation, beginning with a perusal of the newspapers in search of any information that might be relevant to the case.

In a most serendipitous turn of events, I found myself presented with an opportunity to unearth further insights into the Duke of Wexford's financial woes. It transpired that a visit to the illustrious institution, the Westminster Bank, would prove to be an invaluable source of information. In order to execute my plan, I meticulously contrived a disguise that would enable me to navigate the halls of the bank without arousing suspicion. Thus, armed with a veneer of anonymity, I ventured forth into the very heart of London's financial district.

As I strode confidently through the imposing doors of the bank, the grandeur of the surroundings was not lost on me. The opulent interior bespoke a sense of authority and stability, a testament to the institution's status as the guardian of the nation's wealth. In the vast, marble-lined hall, men of consequence hurried about their business, their faces etched with the gravity of their undertakings.

Resisting the urge to gawk at the splendour around me, I made my way to the inner sanctum of the bank, where the fates of men and empires were decided. My carefully crafted disguise as an esteemed banker allowed me to gain entry with nary a second glance from the guards who stood sentinel at the entrance. Once inside, I began my search for information pertaining to the Duke of Wexford's financial affairs.

In the maze of offices and chambers that comprised the bank's inner workings, I surreptitiously delved into the records and correspondence concerning the Duke of Wexford's financial transactions. My diligence was rewarded as I unearthed a trove of disconcerting revelations, painting a bleak picture of the Duke's once-robust financial empire, now teetering on the brink of ruin.

It appeared that the Duke had embarked upon a series of ventures with a boundless optimism that had ultimately proved to be his undoing. The investments, once heralded as the very epitome of innovation and progress, had faltered one after another, ensnared in a morass of failed promises and poor management. One of which was an investment in a scheme originated by none other than the disgraced inventor Marcel Merquin himself. As each venture crumbled, the Duke's wealth dwindled, consumed by the inexorable advance of his mounting debts.

As I delved deeper into the Duke's financial quagmire, I uncovered evidence of desperate attempts to salvage his fortune. He had thrown himself into a myriad of speculative ventures, seemingly undeterred by the spectre of failure that had haunted his previous undertakings. Alas, each endeavour proved to be as fruitless as the last, ensnaring the Duke in an growing web of insolvency from which there appeared to be no escape.

In the course of my investigations, I chanced upon several correspondences between the Duke and various financiers, the content of which revealed the extent of his desperation. In florid prose, he beseeched them for assistance, imploring them to grant him the funds necessary to extricate himself from the abyss of financial ruin.

Having obtained the information I sought, I deemed it prudent to take my leave of the Westminster Bank, lest my subterfuge be discovered. In the guise of a weary banker burdened by the weight of his responsibilities, I slipped out of the establishment, my heart heavy with the knowledge of the Duke's plight.

As I pondered the fate of the Duke of Wexford, I could not help but be reminded of the capricious nature of fortune, and how the wheel of fate can turn with such cruel indifference, casting even the mightiest of men into the depths of despair. It was a sobering thought, and one that served as a reminder that even the seemingly invincible can fall victim to the whims of fate.

In the quiet solitude of my lodgings, I reflected on the revelations I had gleaned from my clandestine visit to the bank. The Duke's tale of financial ruin and desperation stood in stark contrast to the glittering façade of wealth and privilege that had once defined his existence. His story served as a poignant reminder of the transitory nature of worldly success, and the ephemeral nature of the things we so ardently pursue.

Yet, even as I contemplated the melancholy fate of the Duke of Wexford, I could not escape the sense that his misfortunes were somehow entwined with the greater tapestry of events that had unfolded throughout the course of my investigation. The tangled skeins of deceit and betrayal that had ensnared the Duke seemed to be connected, in some as yet unfathomable manner, to the machinations of those who had sought to exploit his vulnerability for their own nefarious ends.

As I mulled over the disparate threads of information that had come to light during our inquiry, I was struck by the realisation that the key to unravelling the mystery lay in understanding the true nature of the connections that bound these seemingly hitherto unrelated events together.

Quiet contemplation, and a lifetime of constructive cynicism, led me to build a hypothesis that the Duke himself may have been involved in the theft of his wife's splendid necklace, fit for a maharaja's favourite concubine, perhaps in a desperate attempt to raise funds and salvage his financial ruin. It was a far more plausible explanation than the fantastical tales of international terrorism that Holmes had concocted, and I felt certain that the truth would soon be revealed.

While Holmes and Watson embarked on their wild goose chase, I began to formulate a plan to discreetly gather further evidence and steer them back on the right track. It was clear that, once again, it would be up to me to ensure that justice prevailed, while the bumbling detective remained blissfully ignorant of my involvement.

I pondered upon my hypothetical connection between the stolen necklace and the Duke's financial woes, so I decided to pay a visit to an old acquaintance of mine at Lloyd's of London. Mr Reginald Thornhill, a senior underwriter, was well-versed in the intricacies of insuring high-value assets, and I believed he might be able to shed some light on the matter.

Upon my arrival at the imposing edifice of Lloyd's of London, I was struck by the palpable air of power and wealth that seemed to emanate from its very walls. Like the Westminster Bank, this grand structure, with its ornate façade and bustling interior, stood as a testament to the financial might of the British Empire, and as I stepped through its hallowed portals, I could not help but feel a sense of awe.

Upon navigating the lavish reception hall, I was greeted warmly by Mr Reginald Thornhill, a distinguished gentleman of middle age. His face, framed by a neatly trimmed beard, was lined with the marks of experience, his eyes keen and perceptive, betraying a mind constantly at work.

"Ah, my dear sir," he exclaimed, extending a hand in greeting. "It is a pleasure to make your acquaintance. I understand that you have been investigating the unfortunate matter of the missing

MacGuffin Diamond necklace. Pray tell, how may I assist you in your inquiries?"

I proceeded to inform Mr Thornhill of my suspicions regarding the Duke of Wexford, and the potential link between the theft of the necklace and the recent misfortunes that had befallen his estate. Mr Thornhill listened intently, his expression a mixture of curiosity and concern.

After a moment's profound contemplation, he responded, "Indeed, the circumstances surrounding the disappearance of the diamond are most peculiar. It so happens that the Duke had insured the item for a sum precisely equal to the amount he has recently lost in ill-advised investments. A most curious coincidence, would you not agree?"

As Mr Thornhill spoke, I could not help but feel a growing sense of unease. The revelation that the value of the insurance policy matched the Duke's financial losses only served to strengthen my conviction that he was somehow involved in the theft.

Mr Thornhill, continued. "It seems," he remarked gravely, "that your suspicions were well-founded. I fear the Duke may have resorted to the most underhanded of means in order to extricate himself from his financial difficulties."

The culmination of this inquiry led me to a most disconcerting conclusion: it appeared almost certain that the Duke of Wexford had orchestrated the theft of the diamond necklace in a desperate bid to restore his lost fortune. Yet, in order to expose this infernal scheme, I would need to gather incontrovertible evidence of the Duke's guilt.

With my confidence in a strong case at its peak, I set to work devising an elaborate ruse to expose the Duke's duplicity and recover the stolen jewels. It was essential that I involve Holmes and the authorities at the right moment, ensuring that the farce would play out to perfection.

I devised a plan to ensnare the Duke and bring his unscrupulous activities to light. The task ahead would be sensitive, but I felt a burning sense of duty to see justice served and to protect the reputation of Lloyd's, an institution that played such a vital role in the financial landscape of our great nation.

With the assistance of Mr Thornhill, I resolved to lay an enticing trap for the Duke, one that would lure him into revealing his involvement in the theft of the MacGuffin Diamond necklace. As our scheme took form, we made ready to set our cunning snare in action. A staged event was to be held at a prestigious London venue, one which the Duke would find difficult to resist attending. With the promise of a magnificent gala, and affluent company, we hoped to draw him out and catch him unawares. Holmes and Watson were naturally included as invited guests of the evening, oblivious to the scheme in play.

But before the event, I had work to do. Using the contacts I employed during the case of the counterfeit painting, I commissioned a unique prop required for my ruse to be convincing and effective. Paying considerably more for a rapid outcome, I came into possession of the requisite component of my plan. The game was afoot!

On the appointed evening, the trap was sprung. The Duke, resplendent in his finery, arrived at the event, utterly oblivious to the web that had been woven around him. As the evening progressed, I grew increasingly confident that our plan would succeed. The Duke, unaware of the watchful eyes upon him, let slip several incriminating remarks, which Holmes missed entirely. However, the noose was tightening around the Duke's neck, and it was only a matter of time before he would be forced to confront the consequences of his actions.

At last, the moment of truth arrived. With my preprepared prop to hand amongst the throng of the guests, the Duke was presented with a replica of the stolen MacGuffin Diamond necklace on the bountiful décolletage of Mrs. Cassandra O'Reilly, who you may remember had assisted me in the previous case. The Duke recoiled, his face a picture of confusion and shock. Recognising his heirloom, he lunged for the jewels, only to knock Holmes sideways, who was stood close to the events as they unfolded, by luck, rather than judgment.

"How can this be?" the Duke yelled. "I have those jewels right here…" The Duke, patting his breast pocket, unexpectedly discovering the tell-tale impression of 20cts of MacGuffin Diamond, and immediately realised his folly as well as the devious trap he had fallen into.

The Duke's visage underwent a profound metamorphosis as he registered the consternation and incredulity that had swiftly taken hold of him. Once an esteemed pillar of high society, he found himself caught in the intricate web of his own maleficent design, his illustrious reputation irrevocably tarnished by the ignominy of his actions. The Duke uttered a strangled gasp, his face betraying the depths of his mortification and despair.

The Duke, cornered and desperate, made for the nearest exit. It was then that the police, plain-clothed and forewarned by an 'anonymous' telegram from myself, blocked the Duke's egress. The arresting officers, embodying justice and propriety, clasped the cold, unforgiving manacles about his delicate wrists, sealing his fate as the mastermind behind the reprehensible events that had transpired. His sordid stratagem, once shrouded in secrecy, was now laid bare for all to witness in its abject degradation.

"Surely, this is some manner of jest, some cruel ploy designed to humiliate and abase me," the Duke exclaimed, his eyes darting about the room in a vain search for some semblance of mercy or understanding. "I am a man of honour and distinction, and I shall not suffer this indignity in silence!"

The lead officer, a stern and unyielding figure, regarded the Duke with a mixture of contempt and pity, his voice firm and resolute as he addressed the beleaguered aristocrat. "Your Grace, I assure you that this is no jest, nor is it an endeavour to besmirch your name unjustly. The evidence against you is both incontrovertible and damning, and it is our solemn duty to see that justice is meted out accordingly."

As the officer continued, the Duke's visage grew increasingly pallid, the last vestiges of his pride and composure crumbling beneath the weight of his impending fate. "You will be held accountable for your transgressions, and you shall be required to face the full weight of the law."

The Duke's eyes widened as the reality of his situation began to truly sink in. His lips trembled and quivered, as though struggling to form some manner of retort or plea, yet ultimately no words emerged from his once eloquent maw. He stood before his accusers, the very image of a man who had been utterly and irrevocably broken by the revelation of his own malfeasance.

It was not long thereafter that the purloined MacGuffin Diamond necklace was recovered from its resting place in the Duke's breast pocket, its resplendent beauty marred only by the taint of the nefarious plot that had sought to lay claim to it. The magnificent gemstone, once the pride of the Duke's ancestors, now stood as a testament to the depths of human greed and avarice, a potent symbol of the perils that lay in wait for those who sought to traverse the treacherous path of deception and villainy.

As the Duke was led away, his once-imposing form now reduced to a pitiable, slumped figure, the onlookers who had gathered could not help but feel a mingling of disgust and pity for the fallen aristocrat. Once a paragon of nobility and virtue, he was now naught but a cautionary tale, a living embodiment of the wages of sin.

The officers, their faces grim and resolute, guided the Duke towards the awaiting carriage that would convey him to his inevitable reckoning. As the carriage door was opened, the Duke cast one final, imploring glance at those who had borne witness to his disgrace, as if to beseech them for some modicum of understanding or forgiveness.

"May Providence have mercy upon my soul," he whispered, his voice scarcely more than a strangled sob as the cold, unyielding door of the carriage was shut behind him. The horses snorted and stamped, their hooves echoing like the tolling of a funeral bell, and the carriage began its slow, inexorable journey towards the halls of justice.

As the carriage receded into the distance, the sombre crowd began to disperse, their whispered conversations carrying the heavy burden of the Duke's downfall. The once-great man had been laid low by his own avarice, his transgressions exposed for all to see. Yet, amidst the scandal and the outrage, there was also a sense of relief, for justice had been served, and the priceless MacGuffin Diamond necklace could now be restored to the bosom of the Duchess, herself a victim of society's judgment.

And so, the curtain was falling on this sordid tale of greed and deception, with justice emerging triumphant in the end. Although Holmes had bumbled his way through the case, making a series of ineffective blunders, the truth had ultimately been revealed, thanks in no small part to my own diligent efforts.

As I returned to my humble abode, I could not help but chuckle to myself, amused by the improbable series of events that had unfolded before my very eyes. Through my cunning, I had ensured that the Duke would be brought to justice and the stolen necklace restored to its rightful owner. All the while, I had allowed the bumbling Holmes to believe that he had been the one to solve the case.

As I settled into my armchair by the window, I poured myself a glass of fine Madeira and reflected on the events of the past few days. I had once again proven myself to be the true master of deduction, effortlessly manipulating events from the shadows while the great Sherlock Holmes stumbled blindly from one ludicrous theory to another.

From my vantage point, I observed Holmes and Watson returning to 221B Baker Street, no doubt eager to regale each other with tales of their daring exploits. As the two of them entered their residence, I could hear the unmistakable sound of Holmes's violin as he began to play a triumphant melody, celebrating another apparently successful investigation.

Despite my satisfaction at having outwitted Holmes once more, I could not help but feel a pang of sympathy for the hapless detective. In his own bumbling way, he was merely attempting to bring a semblance of justice to the world. Nevertheless, it was clear to me that the realm of criminal investigation was far better served by our unique partnership.

As I continued to observe the comings and goings of Baker Street, I knew that it would not be long before another perplexing case would present itself, and once again, I would be called upon to demonstrate my superior skills of deduction. For now, however, I could content myself with the knowledge that I had once more succeeded in outmanoeuvring the great Sherlock Holmes, ensuring that justice was served and maintaining the delicate balance between good and evil in the bustling metropolis of our great city, London.

In the meantime, I would keep my watchful eye on my unsuspecting neighbours, always ready to intervene should the need arise. As the sun began to set over the city, I raised my glass in a silent toast to my latest victory, savouring the sweet taste of success and the knowledge that, for now at least, the streets of

London were a little safer thanks to the covert efforts of Horatio Ollerenthorpe.

Chapter 8: The Phantom Stagecoach

A dreary morning in October found me once again at my usual post by the window, observing the comings and goings of Baker Street. The sound of horses' hooves and the creaking of carriage wheels echoed through the damp air, as the city awoke to face another day of toil and struggle. My keen eyes watched the passers-by, ever vigilant for any signs of criminal activity or intrigue that might call upon my skills of deduction.

As I sat sipping my morning cup of tea, I noticed a carriage pulling up in front of 221B. From within emerged a tall, elegant lady, her face concealed beneath the veil of her hat. I could tell from her graceful gait and the way she carried herself that she was a woman of high breeding and accustomed to the finer things in life. With a gloved finger to her lips, she hesitated for a moment before ascending the steps to the door and rapping on it with her gloved hand. Billy opened the door and granted the visitor entry.

I could not resist the urge to eavesdrop on the conversation that followed, straining my ears to catch every word as Holmes and Watson welcomed their newest client into their abode.

"Pray, be seated, madam," said Holmes, likely gesturing towards an armchair. "You have come to seek my assistance in a matter most urgent and distressing, I perceive."

The lady hesitated, no doubt casting a nervous glance around the room. "Indeed, Mr Holmes," she began, her voice trembling with emotion. "I am Lady Agatha Montmorency, and I fear that my family has fallen victim to a most sinister and mysterious occurrence."

As is his custom, Holmes could not help himself using this as an impromptu opportunity to display his deductive prowess to impress the anxious lady and put her at ease. "Now madam, I perceive that you have travelled from the countryside, most likely from a grand estate located near a river. You dine frequently at

Claridge's and were recently a visitor to the British Museum." he announced confidently.

Lady Agatha looked puzzled. "Well, no, Mr Holmes, our estate is located in the West London. I have never dined at Claridge's, on account of its distasteful patronisation by the proletariat and foreign nobility. As for the British Museum, I care not for it."

Undeterred by this blatant error, Holmes continued, "And you have come by train, judging by the slight disarray of your hat and the flecks of soot upon your gloves."

"Again, I am afraid you are mistaken, sir," Lady Agatha replied, a touch of annoyance creeping into her voice. "I travelled here entirely by carriage, as you might well have observed."

The hapless detective, clearly flustered, attempted to regain his composure. "Ah, well, no matter. Pray, continue with your tale, Lady Agatha."

Lady Agatha sighed, clearly unimpressed with Holmes's performance thus far. "Very well. You see, Mr Holmes, my family has long been plagued by a legend of a phantom stagecoach that appears on the grounds of our estate every full moon. It is said to be driven by a long-deceased ancestor; a ghostly figure clad in black, and those who see it are fated to meet a terrible end. These last three months have seen an escalation in the violence and destruction perpetrated by this ghoul, and I fear for the lives of my husband and I, as it is soon to be a full moon once again."

Holmes scoffed at the notion, confidently waving a hand with a flourish. "Fear not, Lady Agatha. I shall unravel this mystery and expose the truth behind this so-called phantom stagecoach."

After the departure of Lady Agatha, I could hear the clumsy steps of Holmes pacing the room, his mind racing as he attempted to piece together the threads of the case. "It is clear to me, Watson, that this phantom stagecoach is no mere coincidence or childish fable. It is, in fact, a cleverly constructed ruse designed to distract the Montmorency family from their true enemies – foreign agents attempting to undermine the British Empire's influence in the Far East!"

Watson furrowed his brow, unconvinced by Holmes's wild theory. "Holmes, old chap, are you quite certain of that? It seems a rather far-fetched notion, even for you."

But the deluded detective would not be swayed. "Trust me, Watson, I have never been more certain of anything in my life! We must travel to Lady Agatha's estate at once and uncover the truth behind this nefarious plot."

Holmes and Watson made quick preparations for their journey to the estate. Their security paramount.

"Watson, I trust you have packed your service revolver?" asked Holmes.

"I always carry it on cases such as this, Holmes." replied Watson, with a pat to his breast pocket.

"Me too this time, my dear fellow." Holmes patting his breast pocket in reply. Never one to heed safety precautions, Holmes' revolver proceeded to fire, the bullet tearing a hole through his cape and ricocheting off a brass spittoon, eventually finding its way into a portrait of Queen Victoria, squarely between the eyes.

With hardly a word exchanged between them, the duo made their final preparations to depart. Their game, afoot.

I could hardly believe the absurdity of Holmes's actions and deductions, but I knew I had to keep a close eye on his investigation lest his incompetence lead him astray. I quickly donned the guise of a hansom cab driver and offered my services for their journey to the Montmorency estate.

As we rattled along the cobblestone streets, I eavesdropped on Holmes and Watson's conversation, which was growing ever more farcical by the moment.

"I tell you, Watson, it all makes perfect sense!" Holmes exclaimed. "These foreign agents have concocted the story of the phantom stagecoach to terrify the Montmorency family into submission, leaving them vulnerable to their evil plans."

Watson attempted to interject, but Holmes ploughed on, growing increasingly excited by his own wild conjectures. "And mark my words, Watson, we shall find evidence of these agents' treachery at the very heart of the Montmorency estate – perhaps even in the form of secret messages hidden in plain sight, disguised as innocent household items!"

The good doctor sighed, resigned to the fact that his friend's imagination had well and truly run away with him. "Very well, Holmes, but let us not jump to conclusions before we have examined the evidence for ourselves."

As the cab rolled on towards the Montmorency estate, I could not help but roll my eyes in disbelief at Holmes's ludicrous theories. But with any luck, my watchful eye and discreet intervention would be enough to steer him back onto the path of truth and justice.

As the cab traversed the threshold of the imposing wrought iron gate that marked the entrance to the Montmorency estate, sunlight burst through the clouds as if mana from heaven. I found myself momentarily struck dumb by the sheer splendour and magnificence of the landscape that unfolded before my very eyes. The estate, an Eden beyond compare, replete with a myriad of horticultural delights, seemed to defy the very confines of reality, its picturesque tableau a testament to the Montmorency family's impeccable taste and boundless resources.

As we progressed along the elegantly manicured gravel path that meandered its way towards the resplendent manor house, our vision was regaled by the sight of an arboretum of such prodigious beauty that it seemed as though it had been conjured from the pages of some fantastical tome. The Japanese Maples, their foliage ablaze with a dazzling spectrum of reds, stood as silent sentinels amidst the verdant expanse, their boughs whispering softly in the gentle breeze that caressed the estate with a tender, almost reverential touch.

Our attention was momentarily diverted by the presence of several flat-capped groundsmen, their countenances furrowed with concentration as they meticulously tended to the immaculate gardens that adorned the estate. The industrious workers moved with a sense of purpose and dedication that bespoke their unwavering commitment to the preservation and enhancement of the Montmorency family's horticultural legacy, their every movement a study in precision and harmony.

From above, I could hear Holmes take a deep intake of breath as he took in the splendour before us, expecting a soliloquy espousing the unfathomable beauty of nature and its skilful control by man.

"Nice, isn't it?" he muttered.

Rolling my eyes again, we continued our journey through the sylvan paradise, we were afforded a glimpse of the myriad flora and fauna that called the estate their home, their very presence serving to elevate the Montmorency grounds to a realm of near-mythical enchantment. The mellifluous song of birds filled the air, their dulcet tones weaving a tapestry of sound that seemed to resonate with the very soul of the landscape. Squirrels and rabbits darted to and fro amidst the underbrush, their playful antics a testament to the vibrant life that flourished within the Montmorency demesne.

As the cab rolled ever onwards, we were regaled by the sight of several meticulously sculpted topiaries, their exquisite forms expertly fashioned into a menagerie of fantastical creatures and whimsical shapes. These horticultural marvels stood as silent guardians of the Montmorency estate, their presence a tribute to the skill and artistry of the dedicated groundsmen who toiled tirelessly to maintain their exquisite forms.

The sun, its golden rays suffusing the landscape with a warm and ethereal radiance, cast dappled shadows upon the verdant lawns, imbuing the scene with a sense of tranquillity and repose that seemed almost otherworldly in its intensity. The air, redolent with the perfume of mid autumn, seemed to caress the senses, as though inviting us to partake in the myriad delights that the Montmorency estate had to offer.

Approaching the manor house, we were greeted by the family butler, Gladstone. He was a tall, wiry fellow with a pallid complexion and a prominent brow that lent him a stern appearance. His eyes darted about nervously, as if he were constantly on the lookout for some hidden danger, and his fingers fidgeted with the buttons of his waistcoat in a most disconcerting manner. Despite his impeccable attire and the polite formality of his speech, it was clear to me that Gladstone was a man with secrets – and I was determined to discover what they might be.

Holmes and Watson were granted entry and introduced to Lord Montmorency, a man with a permanent frown and serious countenance clearly not to be trifled with. Meanwhile, I set about work by first hiding the cab discreetly behind a copse of trees. I resolved to adopt the semblance of a chimney sweep, thereby granting me the liberty to traverse the manor with impunity and devoid of scrutiny, akin to the manner in which all guttersnipes are customarily regarded by our callous and unfeeling society.

As the day wore on, I knew it would fall to me to unravel the true mystery of the phantom stagecoach and expose the secrets that lurked within the Montmorency estate. Armed with my wits and my trusty broom, I prepared to embark on a thrilling adventure that would no doubt leave Sherlock Holmes once again scratching his head in bafflement.

I began my investigations throughout the Montmorency estate, gathering crucial pieces of evidence that would undoubtedly bring the truth to light. My first discovery was a letter tucked away in Lady Agatha's vanity, penned by her physician. The letter revealed, much to my astonishment, that the poor woman was, in fact, barren; a secret she had kept hidden from her husband and the rest of the world.

With this newfound knowledge in hand, I turned my attention to the enigmatic butler, Gladstone. After some time, I managed to slip into his quarters undetected, only to find a series of letters exchanged between Gladstone and his mother. These missives painted a most intriguing picture – that Gladstone was not merely a servant in the Montmorency household, but rather the illegitimate offspring of Lord Montmorency's own father.

The pieces of the puzzle were beginning to fall into place. It was clear to me that Gladstone, knowing of his true parentage and desperate to claim his birth right, had concocted the tale of the phantom stagecoach to drive Lord and Lady Montmorency either from their estate or into the grave. With the couple out of the way, Gladstone could step forward and assert his claim to the family fortune.

I ventured to the outbuildings of the estate, seeking further evidence to solidify my case against Gladstone. After an exhaustive search, I stumbled upon an old stagecoach hidden away in a dusty barn. The sight of the vehicle sent shivers down my spine, for it was none other than the ghostly apparition that had terrorised the Montmorency estate. Perched atop the driver's seat, I discovered a long, black cloak and a ghastly mask. Inside the stagecoach, a tin pot containing phosphor. The perfect tools to complete Gladstone's deceitful ruse.

As I scurried about the manor, blackened and sooty, I overheard Holmes and Watson discussing their strategy for the evening. They were gathered in the drawing-room, their voices hushed and conspiratorial.

"It is as I suspected, Watson!" Holmes declared with a wild gleam in his eye. "The full moon tonight will provide the perfect cover for those foreign agents to carry out their dastardly plot. We must be prepared to apprehend them in the act!"

Watson sighed, clearly unconvinced. "Holmes, have you considered that perhaps you're reading too much into this situation? It could simply be a matter of the family being frightened by local superstition and happenstance."

But Holmes would not be deterred. "Nonsense, Watson! There are dark forces at work here, mark my words, and we must root them out. Tonight, we shall lie in wait and catch these miscreants red-handed!"

As the two men continued to plan their ill-conceived stakeout, I could not help but chuckle at the absurdity of their conclusions. It was obvious to me that they were chasing shadows, while the true culprit – the shifty butler, Gladstone – remained in their midst, unobserved.

In possession of crucial evidence, I resolved to bring an end to Gladstone's dreadful plot. But first, I needed to devise a plan that would expose the butler's true intentions, while also ensuring that the bumbling Holmes would not inadvertently disrupt my efforts. And so, with a wry smile on my lips, I began to set the stage for a dramatic confrontation that would leave the great detective utterly confounded.

Returning to the outbuilding where I discovered the wretched apparatus of Gladstone's monstrous scheme, I applied a slender coating of phosphor upon the interior of the mask, thereby laying a cunning snare for the artful butler. Little would Gladstone know that the very instruments of his stratagem would prove to be his own downfall. Having laid the trap, the only requisite was to let events unfold.

With most of the estate's industrious staff destined for home or the local public house, dusk began to settle, and the gloaming deepened. Holmes and Watson took up their places for their misguided stakeout. Holmes sported his customary deerstalker cap, as epitomised in Watson's exaggerated accounts, albeit worn sideways by the imbecile.

The Montmorency estate lay shrouded in an air of anticipation. The darkness that enveloped the grounds seemed to hold its breath, waiting for the arrival of the spectral stagecoach that had so captivated the minds of the local populace. I, concealed within the shadows of a nearby copse, observed with bated breath as the appointed hour approached.

It was then that the spectral stagecoach made its appearance, the ghostly apparition materialising from the depths of the darkness like a malevolent wraith. The very air around it seemed to quiver with dread, as though recoiling from the sinister emanations of its otherworldly presence. The stagecoach, bathed in an eerie luminescence, glided through the estate, its ghostly horses snorting and pawing at the earth, their hooves tympanic upon the ground.

Holmes, with the naïve enthusiasm of a schoolboy embarking upon a great adventure, burst out from his hiding place and positioned himself in the path of the approaching apparition, ready to spring his ill-conceived trap. Watson, ever the loyal companion, stood close by, his face a picture of trepidation and uncertainty as he gazed upon the approaching spectre.

As the ghoulish equipage approached, Holmes, his eyes ignited with exhilaration, surged towards the otherworldly conveyance, his upper limbs extended in a vain endeavour to seize the impalpable apparition. Alas, in his ardour to ensnare the evasive wraith, the flap upon Holmes' deerstalker chapeau became unfastened, folding downwards to occlude his line of sight. Providentially for him, he blundered upon an invisible root and, in consequence, went hurtling headfirst into a thicket.

The force of his ungainly plunge sent a cacophony of rustling and snapping through the foliage, as branches and twigs protested his unceremonious intrusion. Watson, alarmed by his friend's misadventure, rushed to his side, casting anxious glances at the spectral stagecoach as it continued its unhindered progress through the estate.

Holmes, emerging from the depths of the hedgerow, his dignity bruised and battered as his physical form, bemoaned his ill fortune and the fickle hand of fate that had conspired to thwart his efforts. His face, a tableau of chagrin and discomfiture, bore the marks of his calamitous encounter with the unyielding shrubbery. Watson, his countenance a mask of concern, assisted his beleaguered companion to his feet and offered what consolation he could muster.

Meanwhile, the phantom stagecoach continued its spectral journey, traversing the grounds of the Montmorency estate with an air of triumph, its ghostly driver laughing derisively at the bungling efforts of the great detective. It recklessly crashed through rows of precious saplings, and destructively churned up aromatic herb gardens as it went.

As it disappeared into the inky blackness of the night, the spectral stagecoach left behind a trail of whispers and sighs, the echoes of its unearthly passage through the haunted domain. The night fell silent once again.

I, having witnessed the entire farcical episode from my secluded vantage point, allowed myself a wry smile at the absurdity of the spectacle. Once again, the great Sherlock Holmes had demonstrated his propensity for blundering into folly and misadventure, his haphazard approach to the investigation proving to be his undoing.

As Holmes and Watson, bruised and crestfallen, retreated from the scene of their ignominious defeat, I turned my thoughts to the task that lay ahead. It was clear that the mystery of the phantom stagecoach will be satisfactorily resolved the next day, by a solution that eschewed the bumbling antics of the great detective in favour of reasoned analysis and careful deduction.

As the first light of dawn began to tint the eastern sky with the pale hues of morning, seizing the opportunity, I slipped a note under Holmes' bedroom door, advising him that the scheming ghoul would unwittingly reveal himself that very day, as dusk falls. With bated breath, I awaited the dawning of a new day, eager to see the fruits of my labour.

Later that morning, Holmes nursed his wounds and pride over a large breakfast of steaming coffee and kedgeree. Whilst Watson tucked into a second plateful, Holmes impatiently began a fruitless search for the phantom stagecoach, missing the resting place of the stagecoach in the old barn entirely.

As evening fell on the Montmorency estate, Gladstone went about his duties, unaware of the impending snare. When the light gradually dimmed, the phosphor I had secreted on the inside of the mask began to glow on Gladstone's face, casting an eerie luminescence across the butler's visage. Holmes, Watson, and the Montmorency family looked on in shock as the true identity of the phantom was unmasked.

"What is the meaning of this?" bellowed Lord Montmorency, enraged by the deception.

The atmosphere in the drawing room of Montmorency estate was laden with tension, the air heavy with the weight of anticipation as the denouement of the ghostly stagecoach mystery drew near. The fire in the hearth flickered and cast erratic shadows upon the walls, illuminating the faces of those present with an eerie, capricious glow.

Holmes, his lanky frame imposing and his gaze piercing, levelled his scrutiny upon the butler, Gladstone, who stood before him with an enigmatic expression. In that moment, the air of calm detachment that had hitherto marked the man's countenance seemed to crack, revealing a hint of the turmoil that roiled beneath the surface.

"Ah, yes," Holmes proclaimed, his voice tinged with a note of triumph that belied the clumsy nature of his recent exploits, "I deduced that you, Gladstone, were indeed the mastermind behind the ghostly stagecoach. It was all an elaborate ruse to drive the Montmorencys from their estate and lay claim to their fortune."

As these words reverberated through the chamber, a palpable shift in the atmosphere occurred, the tension escalating to a fever pitch as the full implications of Holmes' accusations sank in. Gladstone's visage, once a mask of inscrutability, now contorted into a snarl of rage and defiance, the depths of his perfidy laid bare for all to see.

"So, my scheme unfolds. No matter. It's about time the truth came out, and my mother and I finally receive our just deserts!"

In an instant, the room erupted into chaos as Gladstone, driven to desperation by the prospect of his imminent downfall, lunged for a decorative sword that hung upon the wall. With a nimble flourish, he brandished the weapon menacingly, his eyes wild with the fervour of a cornered animal.

Holmes, taken aback by this sudden turn of events, scrambled to find a suitable means of defence. His eyes fell upon a poker that lay beside the hearth, its iron shaft gleaming in the firelight, the handle adorned by a decorative head of a gun dog. With the grace of a new-born colt, he snatched up the implement and brandished it in a manner that suggested he was more likely to trip over his own feet than land a decisive blow.

The ensuing battle was as farcical as it was suspenseful, the two combatants engaging in a clumsy dance that bore little resemblance to the elegant art of fencing. Their movements, punctuated by the clang of metal on metal and the occasional grunt of exertion, were a curious blend of desperation and ineptitude, a spectacle that would have been laughable were it not for the high stakes involved.

As the contest raged on, it became clear that victory would not be decided by skill or cunning, but rather by sheer, unadulterated luck. And so it was that Holmes, in a moment of fortuitous clumsiness, managed to disarm his opponent with an ungainly swing of his poker, sending the sword clattering to the ground.

Gladstone, bereft of his weapon and faced with the prospect of imminent defeat, surrendered with a mixture of disbelief and resignation.

Within the hour, he was led away in shackles by the local constabulary, his expression bore the marks of a man who had been outwitted by the most improbable of adversaries.

The room, now devoid of the tumult that had so recently filled it, was left in a state of disarray, the aftermath of the battle a testament to the preposterous nature of the encounter. Holmes, his dignity bruised but intact, surveyed the scene with a measure of satisfaction, the clumsy triumph a fitting conclusion to an absurd and farcical affair.

Summoning a tone of grandiloquence and assuring himself that Watson had his notebook at the ready, Holmes embarked upon a bombastic monologue, regaling his audience with the ostensibly prodigious feats of deduction that had led him to the unmasking of Gladstone. "My dear compatriots," he began, his voice resounding with an air of self-congratulation, "allow me to elucidate the extraordinary process of ratiocination that has culminated in the resolution of this most perplexing and absurd affair.

"Through the application of my keen intellect and the assiduous observation of the minutest details," he continued, his countenance suffused with an air of self-satisfaction, "I was able to discern the subtle connections and seemingly innocuous clues that inexorably led me to the identification of the malefactor at the heart of this confounding enigma. It was a *tour de force* of cerebral acuity, a masterful demonstration of the formidable powers of deduction that have earned me such renown and distinction."

Emphatically delivered, but devoid of any specific details, the soliloquy came to an end. Holmes nodded to himself with an air of satisfaction and extracted his pipe from his pocket.

In spite of the preposterous assertions made by Holmes, purporting to have singlehandedly unravelled the complex threads of the case, the truth had, fortuitously, been brought to light. The beleaguered Montmorency family could, at last, breathe a collective sigh of relief, their lives no longer plagued by the spectre of criminality that had heretofore hung over their noble lineage.

The evildoer Gladstone, the architect of the family's tribulations, was apprehended and detained, his machinations thwarted by the timely intervention of justice. The gruesome mask, the ill-fated stagecoach, and the butler's ill-conceived aspirations of grandeur were all consigned to the annals of history, their sinister influence now permanently expunged from the lives of the Montmorency family.

As the illustrious Montmorency estate gradually returned to a state of tranquillity and order, an ineffable sense of satisfaction welled up within me, buoyed by the knowledge that I had played a pivotal role in the resolution of the case, albeit from the shadows.

Once more, I had succeeded in unmasking the truth and restoring the balance of justice, while the great Sherlock Holmes stumbled and fumbled his way through yet another farcical misadventure. Oblivious to the clandestine assistance he had received, Holmes continued to bask in the adulation of the masses, his reputation as London's foremost consulting detective seemingly unassailable.

As I stood there back in Baker Street, gazing out upon the bustling streets of London, I could not help but reflect upon the curious and oftentimes absurd circumstances that had led me to this juncture in my life. The path I had chosen was not one of fame or fortune, but rather a silent and unheralded crusade for truth and justice, my efforts destined to remain forever shrouded in secrecy. Yet, in the quiet recesses of my heart, I knew that my work had not been in vain, and I resolved to continue my covert endeavours, ever watchful and vigilant, as the unseen guardian of justice in the heart of the great metropolis.

Chapter 8: The (Mis)Adventure of the Duplicitous Diplomat

It was a foggy autumn day in London when I overheard the latest case to fall upon the doorstep of 221B Baker Street. After a knock at the door, Mrs. Hudson ushered in a well-dressed gentleman, carrying himself with an air of importance. Through the window, I overheard the conversation between the client, Sherlock Holmes, and Dr Watson.

"Good day, gentlemen," the man began, his voice laden with a foreign accent. "My name is Mr Henrik van de Velde, and I am the attaché to the Ambassador of the Netherlands. I come to you with a matter of grave importance."

Holmes, ever confident in his deductive abilities, was true to form. "Ah, Mr van de Velde, I can deduce that you have come from north London, travelling by hansom cab, and you are most certainly a vegetarian."

The diplomat scoffed. "Mr Holmes, I am impressed by your skills, but you are mistaken. I have come from the west of your fine city, travelled by foot, and I am an avid meat-eater, often enjoying the flesh of exotic creatures from across the Dutch Empire."

Holmes, sounding rather perturbed but never one to admit defeat, moved the conversation onwards. "No matter, Mr van de Velde. Please tell us about your case."

The attaché explained that a valuable dossier, containing sensitive diplomatic information, had gone missing from the embassy. The loss of this dossier could potentially damage diplomatic relations between the Netherlands and England.

As the trio stood in the dimly lit sitting room, Holmes took a surprising approach to addressing Mr van de Velde's plight. "Mr van de Velde," Holmes declared, his voice dripping with condescension, "I believe you have not been entirely truthful with us. Your body language betrays you. You have not lost the dossier in some dastardly theft but have simply misplaced it!"

Dr Watson, ever the voice of reason, tried to interject. "Holmes, I think you might be jumping to conclusions. We should at least investigate the embassy before making such accusations."

But Holmes would not be swayed. "Nonsense, Watson! I am sure of it. Mr van de Velde, I suggest you return to your embassy and conduct a thorough search. You will find the dossier right under your nose!"

The Dutch diplomat, taken aback by Holmes' accusations, huffed indignantly. "Mr Holmes, I assure you that we have searched every nook and cranny of the embassy. The dossier is nowhere to be found. I implore you to reconsider."

Unwilling to let Holmes' bumbling foolishness derail the investigation, I decided to take matters into my own hands. While Holmes busied himself with wild conjectures and baseless accusations, clearly his mind made up, I would conduct a proper investigation of the embassy and uncover the truth behind the missing dossier. With Holmes and Watson none the wiser, I set out to unravel the true mystery behind the missing documents and once again save the day from the buffoonery of the great detective.

The next day, I arrived at the embassy, having already donned my disguise as an industrialist in the business of importing fresh flowers from the continent. My forged documents from Robert Gascoyne-Cecil, 3rd Marquess of Salisbury and British Foreign Secretary, were expertly crafted and would surely gain me entry.

As I entered the embassy, I was struck by its grandeur. The hallway boasted a marble floor, gilded mirrors, and ornate chandeliers. The walls were adorned with exquisite tapestries and oil paintings of Dutch landscapes. The air was filled with the delicate scent of fresh tulips, a testament to the nation's famed flower industry.

Upon being escorted to Mr van de Velde's office, I was immediately struck by its meticulous organisation. The diplomat's desk was polished to a gleaming shine, with not a single paper out of place. A row of perfectly aligned fountain pens sat next to an inkwell, a testament to Mr van de Velde's exacting nature.

The diplomat greeted me warmly. "Ah, Mr Cecil's representative, I presume? I am delighted to make your acquaintance. How can I assist you in your business endeavours?"

I smiled congenially and handed him the forged documents. "Mr van de Velde, as an importer of fresh flowers, I have been instructed by Mr Cecil to discuss a potential partnership with your esteemed nation. I trust this matter is of equal importance to you, considering the value of the trade."

Mr van de Velde examined the documents carefully, his eyes betraying no hint of suspicion. "Indeed, it is a matter of great interest to us. Please, have a seat, and let us discuss this further."

As we conversed, I observed Mr van de Velde's impeccable manners and attention to detail. The diplomat's fastidiousness made it all the more improbable that he would have simply misplaced the dossier. I knew that I must uncover the true cause of its disappearance, lest Holmes' half-witted ignorance to allow the matter to slip through the cracks.

Throughout our conversation, I subtly steered the topic towards the security of the embassy and the measures taken to protect sensitive documents. Mr van de Velde, proud of his nation's diligence, eagerly divulged the intricate security protocols in place. Armed with this knowledge, I knew I was one step closer to solving the mystery of the missing dossier and, once again, saving the day from the farcical antics of Sherlock Holmes.

As our conversation drew to a close, Mr van de Velde mentioned something in passing that caught my attention. "By the way, you may have noticed the fresh paint in the hallway. We recently had the embassy redecorated. A new beginning, as they say."

Seizing the opportunity to gain more information, I replied. "Indeed. I hear that Mr Cecil is considering a full redecoration of his offices. Pray, which esteemed establishment is to be credited for the execution of this consummate undertaking?"

"It was Masterpiece Interiors, I am led to believe."

I made a mental note of this information and thanked Mr van de Velde for his time. "Thank you for the enlightening discussion, sir. I will relay our conversation to Mr Cecil. I'm sure he will be most pleased."

Upon leaving the embassy, I decided to investigate the firm responsible for the redecoration, Masterpiece Interiors. I learned that they had an excellent reputation for their craftsmanship and attention to detail. However, upon further digging, I discovered that the owner, one Mr Tobias Finch, had recently disappeared under mysterious circumstances. This raised my suspicions, and I resolved to share my findings with Holmes, albeit discreetly.

Later that evening, I slipped a note under Holmes' door detailing my discoveries. From the safety of my own room, I pressed a glass to the wall, enabling me to listen in on Holmes and Watson as they discussed the new information.

"Ah, Watson, it seems a mysterious benefactor has provided us with most helpful data that leads me to reconsider taking on Mr van de Velde's curious case," Holmes said with an air of bemusement. "It appears the embassy has recently been redecorated, and the owner of the firm responsible has vanished without a trace. How very peculiar, wouldn't you say?"

Watson, reasonable to a tee, replied, "Indeed, Holmes. This could very well be related to the missing dossier. Perhaps we should investigate this further."

As I listened to their conversation, I couldn't help but feel a sense of satisfaction. Once again, I had provided the bumbling duo with a crucial lead that they would undoubtedly misconstrue. Nevertheless, I knew that with my guidance, even the most farcical investigation stood a chance of reaching a successful conclusion.

The following day, Holmes despatched a telegram to Mr van de Velde, confirming his acceptance of the case, and then got straight to work. The inept duo of Holmes and Watson set off to the offices of Masterpiece Interiors, hoping to glean more information about the missing owner and any possible connection to the stolen dossier. From my window, I observed them hailing a cab, dressed in their usual outlandish disguises.

Meanwhile, I decided to investigate the matter further on my own. After discreet enquiries, I headed to the home of Mr Tobias Finch, hoping to find some clue as to his whereabouts. Upon arriving, I discovered the front door ajar. Cautiously, I entered the residence, noting the signs of a hasty departure.

As I rummaged through Finch's belongings, I stumbled upon a collection of letters hidden in a secret compartment in his desk. The letters, partially written in code, seemed to be communication with a mysterious figure who was coercing Finch into stealing the dossier during the embassy's redecoration. The plan had been to use his access to the building as a cover for his criminal activities.

I quickly transcribed the coded letters and returned to my lodgings, where I sent an anonymous telegram to Holmes with my findings. Once again, I used my glass to listen to Holmes and Watson discussing the new information.

"Holmes, this anonymous informant has provided us with what could be a vital clue," Watson exclaimed. "It seems Mr Finch may have been coerced into stealing the dossier while working at the embassy."

Holmes stroked his chin, lost in thought. "Yes, Watson, it appears our case is becoming more tangled by the minute. We must endeavour to unravel this web of intrigue and recover the stolen dossier before it's too late."

As Holmes and Watson continued to muddle through the case, I couldn't help but smirk at their bumbling efforts. Little did they know that I was the one pulling the strings, guiding them toward the truth despite their foolish blunders. And so, the farcical dance continued, with the great Sherlock Holmes none the wiser.

Time, that relentless and inexorable march, pressed upon me with an urgency that left no room for hesitation. The stolen dossier, a matter of paramount importance, demanded my immediate attention and unflagging dedication. I knew that I must act with alacrity and dispatch to locate Mr Finch and retrieve the purloined documents. It was likely a task fraught with peril, yet I remained undaunted, spurred onward by the knowledge that the fate of countless individuals hung in the balance.

For the next part of this investigation, I enlisted the help of Miss Arabella McDonald, the expert codebreaker. Our task began with a thorough examination of the series of letters, cryptic missives that held the key to the whereabouts of Mr Finch and the elusive dossier. These letters, penned in a cipher so complex and abstruse that it would have confounded lesser minds, presented a challenge of prodigious proportions. Yet, imbued with a sense of steadfast determination, we set about the arduous process of decoding the perplexing messages, our faculties sharpened by the exigencies of the situation.

For hours, we toiled with an unrepenting focus, surrounded by a tumultuous sea of papers, the flickering light of a gas lamp casting its glow upon the parchment before me. My fingers, stained with ink and cramped from the exertions of our labours, traced intricate patterns across the page as we sought to unravel the tangled skein of the cipher. The task was both mentally and physically taxing, but we refused to yield to the siren call of respite, for I knew that each passing moment brought the criminals one step closer to achieving their odious objectives.

At long last, after countless hours of painstaking work, the veil of obscurity began to lift, and the true meaning of the coded messages began to coalesce in my mind. The letters, it seemed, contained a wealth of information, a treasure trove of secrets that painted a vivid picture of the clandestine dealings between Mr Finch and the enigmatic figure that lurked in the shadows.

Of particular interest, nestled amidst the intricate web of deceit, was the revelation of a secret rendezvous between the two conspirators. The location, a disreputable establishment in the old rookery of Limehouse, was clearly chosen for its anonymity and its seclusion, a haven for those who sought to conduct their affairs beneath the watchful gaze of the law.

With a clear objective, I knew that I had but a single opportunity to apprehend Mr Finch and recover the stolen dossier. The secret meeting, scheduled to take place under the cloak of darkness, would provide the perfect opportunity to confront the miscreants and put an end to their machinations. With the weight of this responsibility bearing down upon my shoulders, I prepared to embark upon my mission, my resolve unwavering and my spirits buoyed by the prospect of success.

After waving goodbye to Miss McDonald in the early hours of the morning, I despatched a telegram to Holmes, warning him about the impending rendezvous. I set forth, guided by the knowledge gleaned from the decoded letters, and arrived at the location of the secret tryst. Concealed in the shadows, I observed Mr Finch nervously pacing back and forth as he awaited the arrival of his contact.

Suddenly, a hooded figure emerged from the darkness, approaching Finch with an air of authority. They exchanged hushed words, and Finch handed over the stolen dossier. The mysterious figure seemed pleased with Finch's work and tossed him a small bag, presumably filled with payment for his services.

Before I could act, I heard the familiar footsteps of Holmes and Watson clumsily approaching the scene in a hurry. No doubt, they had received my anonymous telegram and were hot on the trail.

As Holmes and Watson burst into the alley, the hooded figure took off, sprinting away with the stolen dossier. Finch, sensing that his time was up, tried to flee as well but was promptly apprehended by the arms of Watson.

Holmes gave chase to the hooded figure, his awkward gait making him appear even more foolish than usual. As the figure darted around the corner that was my own vantage point, I took my chance, using my own agility to outmanoeuvre Holmes and snatch the dossier from the figure's grasp. The hooded figure slipped away into the night.

With the dossier safely in my possession, I melted back into the shadows, whereas Holmes returned to Watson to interrogate Finch.

"Mr Finch," Holmes began, his voice imbued with the solemn gravity that accompanied such weighty matters, "we find ourselves requiring your assistance in ascertaining the identity of the elusive, hooded figure who has thus far managed to elude my most scrupulous and assiduous investigations. Furthermore, we seek information pertaining to the current whereabouts of the purloined dossier, a matter of utmost urgency and importance."

Tobias Finch, his eyes darting about the alley with the skittishness of a cornered animal, appeared to weigh the consequences of his response, the tension in the air growing palpable as Holmes and Watson awaited his reply with bated breath. After considering his fate, Mr Finch spoke, his voice quavering and tremulous, as though each word were a struggle to release from his constricted throat.

"Gentlemen," he began, "I must confess that I am utterly and unequivocally ignorant of the matters to which you allude. I am but a simple craftsman, compelled to conduct the theft of said dossier by persons I am not at liberty to disclose. I assure you; my only aim is to live my life in peace and the comfort of my family, far removed from the evildoings that you describe."

Holmes, his piercing gaze never once wavering from the countenance of Tobias Finch, arched a quizzical eyebrow, as though attempting to ascertain the veracity of the man's protestations. Watson, ever the stalwart companion, furrowed his brow in consternation, his mind no doubt awash with a myriad of possibilities and conjectures.

"Mr Finch," Watson interjected, his voice tinged with a hint of impatience, "we have reason to believe that you possess knowledge that may prove invaluable in our pursuit of justice. I beseech you, sir, to cast aside any reticence or fear that may bind you and speak the truth, for it is only through the revelation of truth that the malefactors who have orchestrated these heinous events may be brought to account."

Tobias Finch, visibly shaken by the gravity of Watson's entreaty, seemed momentarily on the verge of capitulation, as though he were poised to divulge the long-sought secrets that had eluded Holmes and Watson thus far. Alas, his resolve ultimately held firm, and he merely shook his head, his visage a mask of sorrow and regret.

"I have told you all I can, gentlemen," he murmured, his voice barely audible above the oppressive silence that now hung over the room like a pall. "You must seek the answers you require elsewhere."

After handing Finch over to the local constabulary, Holmes and Watson returned to Baker Street, chattering about the events that unfolded that evening.

Back in my rooms, I carefully wrapped the dossier in brown paper and tied it securely with a piece of twine. Next, I wrote a short note to Mr van de Velde, explaining the return of his stolen property without revealing my true identity. I then hailed a trustworthy courier, instructing him to deliver the package directly to the diplomat's hands at the embassy. As the courier rode off into the night, I felt a sense of satisfaction, knowing that I had successfully resolved yet another case, all while remaining an unseen force behind the escapades of Sherlock Holmes.

Later, from my window, I observed a carriage pull up and a certain Mycroft Holmes disembarked, his face red with anger. Rapping on the door of 221B with the full might of the portly figure, he was granted entry by Mrs Hudson. Thundering up the stairs, I heard Mycroft burst through the door of Holmes' sitting room and bellow obscenities the likes of which you only hear in army barracks.

"Have you any idea of what you have done this time, Sherlock, you bungling fool?" Mycroft's mouth no doubt projecting spittle.

"Pray, dear brother, impart to me your accusation and I will retort forthwith!" Holmes replied.

"You've thwarted my scheme to obtain vital documents that threaten Anglo-Dutch relations. My agent reports that you attempted to intervene in a private exchange this very evening, and the documents I have been so desperate to acquire were whisked away into the night! A Dutch diplomat recently had

161

obtained scandalous documents pertaining to the private affairs of the English ambassador in the Hague. Those very documents I had contrived to be purloined by the Mr Finch you so expertly detained! They were to be in my custody at this very moment! That is, until you came along and blew my plans to smithereens!"

With deference to his brother, Holmes hung his head low, but only briefly. "Fear not, dear brother, a plan is already in motion that will see you united with that dossier, and the reputation of our ambassador preserved."

"Well, you better bloody well do, dear brother, or failure will surely spell the end of a dear friend and capable diplomat's career." And with that, Mycroft Holmes stormed out, not before theatrically slamming the door to Holmes' sitting room.

In shock, I contemplated my personal involvement in the inadvertent disruption of Mycroft's plan. In my own narcissistic assumption of the wrongdoing of the mysterious figure, I had mistakenly returned the threatening documents back to the very mastermind of the affair, one I had been foolishly working to assist.

Watson looked perplexed. "But Holmes, what are we to do now? How can we retrieve the dossier once more and prevent disaster?"

Holmes stopped pacing and stared out the window, lost in thought. "It is a most delicate situation, Watson. We must tread carefully, for any misstep could have dire consequences. We shall need to devise a plan to extract the dossier from Mr van de Velde's grasp without alerting him to our intentions."

As the two continued to discuss their strategy, I could not help but feel responsible for the dangerous predicament we now faced. I resolved that I must take matters into my own hands once more to ensure the safety of an English ambassador's reputation and thwart the schemes of the duplicitous Mr van de Velde.

Having listened to Holmes and Watson, I knew that it was imperative to draw Mr van de Velde out of hiding. I considered my options and decided that exploiting his appetite for power would be the most effective course of action.

In an effort to entice Mr van de Velde out of sanctuary and retrieve the dossier, I devised an elaborate ruse, one that would be nigh impossible for the ambitious man to resist. Drawing upon my considerable knowledge of the political climate of our fair city, I fabricated a most tantalising bait: a series of convincing, yet entirely fictitious, telegrams detailing the alleged unearthing of highly valuable information that, if obtained, would place Mr van de Velde in an even more powerful position.

The content of the alleged information pertained to scandalous accounts of infidelity by none other than the British Prime Minister himself. In a society where reputation and propriety were held in high esteem, such a revelation would have the power to topple the very foundations of the British government, leaving it vulnerable to manipulation and control. It would be of immense interest to Mr van de Velde, a man whose insatiable appetite for power and influence was now so painfully apparent; a worthy exchange for the stolen dossier.

In the telegrams, I meticulously arranged for a secret meeting at a secluded location, where the exchange of this ostensibly valuable information would transpire. I had little doubt that Mr van de Velde would be unable to resist the temptation of such a tantalising offer. The potential to wield control over the British government and to manipulate the highest levels of power would be an irresistible lure to a man of his ambitions.

With the bait expertly set, I turned my attention to preparing for the encounter. I knew that if my plan were to succeed, I would need to be at my most resourceful and vigilant, for Mr van de Velde was a formidable adversary, and any misstep on my part could have dire consequences. And so, with a steely resolve and a keen sense of anticipation, I embarked upon the final stage of my stratagem, determined to bring Mr van de Velde to justice and restore order to the beleaguered political institution.

It was with great trepidation and anxiety that I conveyed the intricacies of my plan to Holmes and Watson, knowing full well that the success of this daring stratagem hinged upon the cooperation of these two indomitable champions of justice. They received my missive with an air of solemnity, cognisant of the grave import of the task that lay before us. With haste, they marshalled Lestrade and a cadre of stalwart constables, men whose unswerving devotion to the cause of law and order was matched only by their unwavering courage in the face of peril.

As the hour of the fateful exchange drew nigh, Holmes, Watson and the members of the constabulary, all assumed their positions, each man concealed within the gloomy recesses of the labyrinthine streets that surrounded the designated meeting place. All except a single senior officer standing and waiting in plain-clothes. I, hidden in the shadows with a panoramic view of where the scene would unfold.

The atmosphere was fraught with tension, the very air seeming to crackle with an electric anticipation, as all awaited the arrival of Mr van de Velde and his villainous cohorts. The occasional shrill cries of bats in flight were the sole sounds to punctuate the stillness.

Presently, I espied the silhouettes of several figures approaching our man, their sinister countenances shrouded by the encroaching shadows of night. I watched, my breath bated and my nerves taut, as the exchange began to unfold before our very eyes. The stolen dossier, that repository of delicate and potentially devastating secrets, was produced, its presence a palpable reminder of the high stakes for which we were playing.

At the precise moment deemed opportune, Lestrade gave the signal from a whistle, and the agents of justice sprang forth from their hiding spots, the element of surprise firmly on their side. The air was rent with the discordant cries of alarm as Mr van de Velde and his henchmen found themselves surrounded, hemmed in on all sides by the grim visages of justice. In their panic and desperation, they drew forth their pistols, those malevolent instruments of death and destruction, and prepared to make their final, defiant stand.

A cacophony of gunfire erupted, the staccato report of the pistols echoing through the night like the peals of some demonic thunder. Bullets whizzed through the air, their lethal trajectories tracing a deadly ballet of violence and chaos. The constables, undaunted by the hail of lead that threatened to engulf them, returned fire with unerring accuracy, their own volleys of shot striking true and laying low the villainous henchmen who sought to oppose them.

Holmes, ever the bungling yet intrepid sleuth, engaged in a frenetic duel with Mr van de Velde himself, the two adversaries locked in a desperate struggle for supremacy. Their pistols barked and roared, the acrid smoke of burnt powder filling the air and stinging the eyes. Yet, in the end, it was Holmes who emerged victorious, his final, mis-placed shot, fired blindly through closed eyes, sent a tree-branch crashing down onto Mr van de Velde's weapon arm, the pistol clattering to the ground and leaving the malefactor at the mercy of his pursuers.

With the thunder of battle silenced and the smoke of conflict dissipating into the night, the tableau of the aftermath revealed itself in stark relief. The fallen forms of the henchmen lay scattered about the cobblestones, their erstwhile leader, Mr van de Velde, standing amidst the carnage, his countenance a mask of bitter defeat. The dossier, that precious trove of intrigue and secrets, was retrieved, its contents now secure from exploitation.

Perfectly timed, a carriage, black as midnight and emblazoned with the sigil of Whitehall, promptly emerged from the mist, and pulled up abruptly by the scene of devastation. A long, steady arm reached out from inside the conveyance and retrieved the fateful dossier from Holmes. Without a word being exchanged, the carriage trundled off.

In the cold, unforgiving light of dawn, Mr van de Velde was led away in irons, his dreams of power and influence shattered upon the anvil of justice. Holmes and Watson stood in the aftermath, their faces etched with the grim satisfaction that comes from a battle hard-won and a foe vanquished. As for me, I remained ever the silent observer, content in the knowledge that my role in unmasking this pernicious plot had not gone in vain.

Holmes and Watson, weary from their exertions, returned to their lodgings at 221B Baker Street, their spirits buoyed by their recent success. Holmes, the dutiful cretin, congratulated himself on a job well done, completely oblivious to the fact that it was my careful planning and execution that had brought the case to a successful conclusion. Watson, his loyal friend, supported Holmes' claims, while I continued to observe from the shadows, satisfied in knowing that the British ambassador's reputation was preserved.

In the days that followed, the newspapers were filled with accounts of the daring escapade, the tale of our confrontation with Mr van de Velde and his criminal cohorts recounted in breathless prose and adorned with lurid illustrations. Yet, amidst the clamour of the headlines and the accolades that were heaped upon Holmes, Watson, and the valiant constables, I remained a nameless, faceless figure, my true role in these events known only to those who had been there to witness them first-hand.

Chapter 9: The Case of the Secret Order

From my vantage point, I observed the arrival of Inspector Lestrade, who looked quite troubled as he entered the sitting room at 221B Baker Street. After being offered tea by Billy, Holmes, ever the showman, immediately attempted to deduce simple facts about Lestrade's arrival.

"Ah, Lestrade! I see that you've been feasting on roast beef, and I deduce, by the ticket stub in your pocket, you have travelled to our fair city on the early express from Edinburgh. From the station, you then came directly to my humble abode by hansom cab. I also deduce that Mrs Lestrade's chronic dandruff has finally begun to clear up." Holmes declared confidently.

Lestrade, bemused, shook his head. "Actually, Mr Holmes, I had fish and chips for lunch, and I walked here from Scotland Yard. The so-called ticket stub is in fact a receipt for my lunch. But astonishingly, you are quite right about the let up of my dear wife's seborrheic affliction."

Holmes, audibly smug to have finally made an accurate deduction, if not by blind luck rather than solid reasoning, shifted his weight forward in triumph. He urged Lestrade to share the details of the case that had brought him to Baker Street.

Lestrade proceeded to describe a grisly murder that had taken place in Chiswick, a small town west of London. Mr Atticus Bromsgrove, an apparently wealthy gentleman, had been found in his home with his throat slashed, and there was no sign of forced entry. The local constabulary was at a loss, and Lestrade had come to Holmes in the hope that his peculiar talents might provide the breakthrough they needed.

As Lestrade laid out the details of the case, Holmes listened intently, his eyes narrowing and his brow furrowing as he attempted to weave together the threads of this gruesome mystery. He leaned forward in his armchair, his fingers steepled under his chin, his piercing gaze fixed upon Lestrade, as if trying to extract every last morsel of information from the harried inspector.

Watson, as always eager to assist, sat nearby with his notebook open on his lap, scribbling down every detail Lestrade provided. He nodded thoughtfully, occasionally interjecting with a pertinent question or offering his own insight into the case. His enthusiasm was palpable, and it was clear that he relished the opportunity to work alongside Holmes on yet another challenging mystery.

Holmes, however, seemed to pay little heed to Watson's contributions. He was a man who prided himself on his keen intellect and singular methods of deduction, and he often appeared to regard Watson's input as little more than background noise, an unfortunate side effect of having a loyal companion.

As Lestrade continued to recount the particulars of the murder, Watson ventured a suggestion about the possible motive behind the crime. Holmes, of course, summarily dismissed Watson's ideas with a wave of his hand and a curt, "No, no, my dear Watson, you are missing the point entirely."

Watson, despite being accustomed to Holmes' brusque manner, sounded momentarily crestfallen. However, he quickly resumed his notetaking, determined to learn from his brilliant friend, even if that meant enduring a certain amount of condescension.

Holmes, for his part, seemed to take a perverse pleasure in shooting down Watson's theories, as if each dismissal only served to further validate his own genius. He continued to listen to Lestrade's account, his mind racing ahead, weaving a web of intricate connections and improbable scenarios that, he believed, would inevitably lead him to the truth.

Once Lestrade had concluded his account, Holmes stood, pacing the room as he pontificated on the possible motives and methods behind the crime. His theories grew increasingly convoluted and improbable, suggesting that the murder was the work of an elaborate conspiracy, perhaps involving an international crime syndicate or a rogue government agent.

I stifled a chuckle as I witnessed Holmes' wild conjectures. It was clear that, once again, it would fall to me to unravel the tangled threads of this sordid affair and see that justice was done.

As Holmes and Watson made their preparations to visit the scene of the crime, I began my own investigation, confident that I would uncover the truth behind this heinous act, while the great Sherlock Holmes continued to blunder about in his usual, comical manner.

I quickly made my way to the street, knowing Holmes' peculiar habit of dismissing the first cab to arrive in favour of the second. As luck would have it, a hansom cab was approaching. I hailed it with a sharp whistle, and the driver pulled to a stop before me. I climbed in, instructing him to take me to Chiswick, West London, with haste.

As the horse-drawn carriage rattled through the busy streets of London, I took a moment to plan my next move. I decided to don the disguise of a police constable, in order to gain access to the crime scene and observe Holmes' bumbling investigation up close.

Upon arriving at the impressive home in Chiswick, I quickly changed into my constable's uniform, adjusting my helmet and tunic for a perfect fit. I approached the house with an air of authority, nodding to the other officers who were guarding the entrance. They took me for one of their own and allowed me to pass without question.

I arrived just in time to witness Holmes and Watson alighting from their cab. Holmes, in his usual manner, strode toward the house with a sense of self-importance, while Watson followed dutifully behind. I took up a position near the doorway, where I could hear their conversation without drawing attention to myself.

As Holmes entered the room where the murder had taken place, he immediately launched into a series of far-fetched theories. He examined the room with great intensity, pointing out various objects as if they held the key to some grand conspiracy. Watson, ever the loyal companion, nodded along, trying to keep up with Holmes' rapid-fire deductions.

It was clear that Holmes was grasping at straws, making connections that existed only in his own imagination. His theories grew more outlandish by the minute, much to the stifled smirks and sideways glances of bemusement by the officers present. As I observed his misguided efforts, I knew that it would be up to me to uncover the truth behind this brutal crime and ensure that justice was served.

As Holmes and Watson continued their investigation, I set to work, examining the scene with a keen eye for detail, determined to find the vital clues that the great detective had so easily overlooked.

From where I diligently stood, I noticed two points of interest that I felt confident were pertinent to the case. The first, a portrait of Atticus Bromsgrove, whose visage displayed an air of inner confidence; the second, a small, overlooked detail on the windowsill - a symbol, scratched into the paintwork, almost imperceptible. It could be a crucial clue that may lead to the true perpetrator. I needed to bring it to Holmes' attention without him realising my interference.

I decided to create a diversion. I pretended to stumble, knocking over a nearby vase. The loud crash caught everyone's attention, and as they turned to look, I surreptitiously pointed at the windowsill with my truncheon.

Holmes, eager to find new evidence, noticed the gesture and rushed over to examine the scratches in the paintwork. His eyes lit up with excitement as he began to weave an elaborate and outlandish theory based on this seemingly insignificant mark.

"My dear Lestrade," Holmes began, turning to the inspector with a grand flourish, "I believe I have deciphered the enigmatic conundrum that has been presented to us. This minuscule abrasion on the windowsill is the lynchpin in a grand scheme, one that undoubtedly extends far beyond the confines of this domicile."

Lestrade raised an eyebrow, clearly intrigued by Holmes' dramatic proclamation. "Go on, Mr Holmes," he urged, waiting to hear more.

Holmes continued, his words becoming increasingly grandiose and convoluted. "You see, Inspector, this infinitesimal scratch can only be the result of a malefactor's ingress, achieved by utilising an implement of extraordinary sophistication, such as a multifaceted skeleton key. It stands to reason that our vile evildoer is a master locksmith, undoubtedly a member of an international guild of criminal artisans, hell-bent on perpetrating audacious larcenies and sinister assassinations throughout the realm!"

Lestrade, initially captivated by Holmes' declaration, now seemed uncertain. "That's quite a theory, Mr Holmes," he said hesitantly, glancing at the small scratch as if trying to comprehend how it could possibly lead to such a far-reaching conclusion.

As I watched the exchange from my concealed-in-plain-sight position, I couldn't help but marvel at Holmes' ability to spin a fantastical tale from the flimsiest of evidence. It was clear that his imagination was running wild once more, and it would be up to me to uncover the true significance of the scratch on the windowsill and bring the real culprit to justice.

Lestrade, visibly perplexed by Holmes' elaborate theory, furrowed his brow, and cleared his throat. "Mr Holmes, while your deduction is most certainly *imaginative*, I must confess that I find it rather difficult to accept. As you are aware, criminals engaged in the act of theft are rarely inclined to commit premeditated murder. The nature of this crime makes me think of an entirely different motive, one that has nought to do with a locksmith, no matter how good they are."

Holmes, momentarily taken aback by Lestrade's challenge, paused to consider his words. He stroked his chin thoughtfully, his eyes narrowing as he contemplated the scene before him. "Inspector," he began slowly, "I concede that your objection has merit. However, I must remind you that the world of criminality is replete with incongruities and unexpected alliances. Perhaps our malefactor has been coerced into this terrible act by a malevolent puppet master, one who seeks to advance his own agenda by exploiting the unique skills of our locksmith."

Lestrade's expression remained dubious, but Holmes pressed on, growing increasingly animated as he spoke. "Picture, if you will, a Machiavellian mastermind, orchestrating a labyrinthine conspiracy from the shadows. A man whose influence extends to every corner of our fair city, manipulating the denizens of the criminal underworld like pawns on a chessboard. It is this man, I posit, who holds the key to unravelling the enigma that has been presented to us today."

As I listened to Holmes' impassioned speech, I could scarcely contain my incredulity. His theory had grown even more outlandish, straying further and further from the actual facts of the case, scant as they were. It was evident that, in his eagerness to construct an elaborate narrative, Holmes had lost sight of the crucial details that would lead us to the truth. It fell to me, once again, to quietly uncover the genuine significance of the evidence before us and guide our investigation back on course.

As I stood amidst the tumult of the crime scene, it occurred to me that the key to understanding this abominable act lay not in the arcane theories proposed by Holmes, but rather in the mundane details of the victim's life. His business affairs, personal relationships, and past indiscretions might hold the answers we so desperately sought. It was with this thought that I resolved to return home and consult my extensive archive of newspapers, in the hope of unearthing some vital clue that had thus far eluded us.

I bid a discreet farewell to the young and unassuming constable with whom I had been conversing and ventured forth into the bustling thoroughfare, my mind teeming with possibilities. The journey back to Baker Street was, by necessity, a circuitous one, as I sought to avoid any chance encounter with Holmes or Watson. I hailed a hansom cab and instructed the driver to take a meandering route, affording me ample opportunity to ruminate upon the case at hand.

Upon my arrival at my residence, I swiftly ascended the stairs to my private study, where my vast collection of periodicals lay in wait. With a quiet determination, I set about my task, poring over countless articles in search of some pertinent detail.

As the hours slipped by, I began to despair of ever finding the information I sought. The dim light from the gas lamps cast eerie shadows across the room, while the steady tick-tock of the antique grandfather clock seemed to mock my futile efforts. My eyes grew heavy, weighed down by the burden of the countless articles I had scanned in search of a clue to Mr Atticus Bromsgrove's murder. The words on the pages began to swim before me, their ink bleeding and blurring together into an indecipherable mass, a murky sea of information from which I could discern no meaningful pattern.

I rubbed my weary eyes, attempting to dispel the tendrils of fatigue that threatened to ensnare me. My once methodical approach to the task had devolved into a frantic and haphazard endeavour, as I grabbed at each new paper with increasing desperation. The room seemed to close in around me, the towering stacks of periodicals leaning precariously, as if poised to topple and bury me beneath their crushing weight.

Just as I was about to abandon my efforts, conceding defeat to the seemingly insurmountable task, a particular headline fortuitously caught my eye: "Prominent Local Businessman Embroiled in Scandal." Next to the headline was a photograph of a man that bore an uncanny resemblance to the portrait of the victim, Mr Atticus Bromsgrove, albeit under the name of a Mr Frederick O'Dell. The picture leapt from the page, a beacon of hope amidst the oppressive darkness that had threatened to engulf me. With a surge of renewed vigour, I delved into the article, my mind hungry for the tantalising prospect of the truth concealed within its paragraphs.

The account detailed the sordid exploits of O'Dell, a man whose public persona had been one of respectability and propriety, but whose private life was rife with deceit and moral turpitude. This businessman, a figure of some standing within the community, had been embroiled in a scandalous affair, his secret liaisons with a woman not his wife now splashed across the pages of the local press. The implications of such a revelation were far-reaching, as the man's enemies and erstwhile allies alike clamoured to exploit his newfound vulnerability.

As I read further, I became increasingly convinced that the victim of our current investigation was none other than the subject of this shocking exposé. Mr Atticus Bromsgrove was undoubtedly the same person named Mr Frederick O'Dell in the newspaper clipping. It appeared that our victim had been involved in this sordid affair, one which had left him vulnerable to blackmail and threats of retribution.

The narrative that unfolded before me was one of greed, ambition, and betrayal. It seemed that the businessman's enemies had sought to extort him, demanding payment and favour in exchange for their silence regarding his illicit activities. But the victim, a man of considerable pride and stubbornness, had refused to acquiesce to their demands, instead choosing to weather the storm of scandal that inevitably followed.

As the sordid tale reached its climax, I could not help but feel a pang of sympathy for the victim, a man ensnared by his own weaknesses and ultimately undone by his refusal to submit to his tormentors. It was a tragic end to a life marred by deception and vice, and yet it provided us with the vital clue we needed to unravel the mystery of his demise. But one matter puzzled me; why the need to use a pseudonym? I would not resolve that puzzle until later in the case.

I was clear that the motive for the murder was far more prosaic than Holmes had surmised. I knew that it was my duty to share this revelation with my esteemed colleague and guide our investigation towards a more rational conclusion. And so, in possession of the knowledge I had gleaned from my research, I prepared to re-join Holmes and Watson in their pursuit of justice.

Feeling rejuvenated by my discovery, I decided to reveal the information to Holmes and Watson at the earliest opportunity. I discreetly placed the newspaper containing the scandalous article within a sheaf of other periodicals, intending for Holmes to come across it in the course of his investigations.

As luck would have it, I found myself with the perfect opportunity to witness the ensuing conversation between Holmes and Watson. From the vantage point of my window, I could hear the pair gathered in the sitting room, as they prepared to pore over the documents I had so carefully curated.

Holmes, true to form, began by making wild conjectures and attempting to piece together the scant clues he had gleaned from the crime scene. It was a ludicrous display of ineptitude, one that would have been comical were it not for the gravity of the situation. Watson, ever the loyal companion, listened with an air of bemusement, occasionally interjecting with a word of caution or a gentle reminder of the facts at hand.

As Holmes continued to flounder in his misguided efforts, I could scarcely contain my anticipation. The moment of revelation was fast approaching, and I eagerly awaited the befuddled expression that would surely cross Holmes' face as he stumbled upon the crucial piece of evidence.

At last, Holmes picked up the newspaper containing the article about the scandal. He began to read aloud, his voice faltering as the significance of the information became apparent. He turned to Watson with a mixture of astonishment and confusion, and the pair engaged in a fervent discussion about the potential implications of the businessman's sordid affair.

Despite the significance of the revelation, the scene that unfolded before me was nothing short of farcical. Holmes, in his characteristic buffoonery, managed to concoct a preposterous theory that somehow involved the businessman's affair, a secret cabal of international assassins, and a plot to disrupt the British Empire's trade routes. Watson, to his credit, tried in vain to steer Holmes back to the realm of reason, but the great detective was utterly committed to his hare-brained hypothesis.

I continued to listen, agog, as Holmes proceeded to outline a convoluted plan to ensnare the malignant assassins. The plan, which involved disguises, elaborate ruses, and an improbable rendezvous atop a moving train, was nothing short of ludicrous. It was clear that Holmes, in his relentless pursuit of the fantastical, had lost all sense of reason.

Watson, bless his patient soul, listened intently to Holmes' scheme, occasionally interjecting with a pointed question or a thinly veiled expression of doubt. Despite his concerns, Watson remained loyal to his friend, agreeing to embark on the madcap adventure in the hopes of unearthing the truth behind the grisly murder.

From the safety of my window, I could only shake my head in disbelief, particularly when the very nature of the clues I had provided him with solved the conundrum of the victim's identity so clearly. It was apparent that Holmes' incompetence would not only hinder the investigation but could potentially put both him and Watson in grave danger. It fell to me, once again, to steer the investigation in the right direction and ensure that justice was served.

And so, as Holmes and Watson embarked on their preposterous escapade, I continued my diligent work, piecing together the puzzle that would ultimately expose the murderer and put an end to the case. Little did they know that the key to solving the mystery lay not in the outlandish theories of a bumbling detective, but in the quiet observations of the unassuming figure at the window.

I had initially been perplexed by the enigmatic symbol I encountered on the window ledge, a peculiar emblem that seemed to emanate an air of secrecy and intrigue. Unwilling to let this potential clue remain shrouded in mystery, I embarked upon a meticulous investigation, determined to ascertain the mark's true significance.

Perusing my extensive collection of tomes and scholarly works, I sought any hint or reference to the mystifying symbol. Alas, my initial endeavours proved fruitless, leaving me disheartened and on the brink of abandoning my search. However, a serendipitous encounter at the local bibliothèque provided the catalyst for a breakthrough.

There, amidst the hallowed halls of knowledge, I happened upon a learned gentleman well-versed in the study of secret societies and their clandestine operations. Introducing myself as a fellow researcher, I cautiously broached the subject of the enigmatic mark, displaying a sketch I had made of the symbol.

My interlocutor, a Mr Chistophus P. Quill, scrutinised the drawing with keen interest before his countenance became suffused with a look of recognition. "Ah," he exclaimed, his voice hushed yet animated, "this is the emblem of a particularly obscure and exclusive fraternity known as the Order of the Sable Serpent."

With rapt attention, I listened as Mr Quill regaled me with tales of the Order's covert activities and their long-standing reputation as powermongers and masters of cunning. The Order, he explained, had been established during the tumultuous reign of King Charles II, and had since been embroiled in numerous scandals, conspiracies, and acts of subterfuge. Their emblem, the sinuous serpent encircling a stylised orb, was synonymous with their commitment to secrecy and their unyielding pursuit of power.

This new information gave me hope in discovering the true meaning of this affair, so I delved deeper into the annals of history, poring over newspaper clippings and scandal sheets that chronicled the Order's involvement in the city's most notorious incidents. Through painstaking research, I discovered a connection between the victim of the Chiswick murder and the Order of the Sable Serpent. The unfortunate gentleman had, it seemed, been a member of this shadowy organisation, having been initiated into their ranks some years prior.

My inquiries soon led me to a disquieting revelation: our tragic victim had been embroiled in some form of bitter dispute with one or more fellow members of the Order. This internecine conflict had been sparked by a scandalous affair, one that had sent shockwaves through the highest echelons of London society. The torrid liaison had left the victim vulnerable to blackmail and retribution, thus sealing his tragic fate.

As the cogs of the mystery fell into place, I could not help but marvel at the convoluted web of deceit and treachery that lay at the heart of this sordid case. The mark on the window ledge was, in truth, a damning testament to the victim's entanglement with the Order of the Sable Serpent and a chilling reminder of the lengths to which the society would go to maintain their secrets and protect their interests.

Having unearthed the true significance of the mysterious symbol, I was now in possession of the key that would unlock the solution to the Chiswick murder. But would the obstinate Sherlock Holmes be amenable to the truth, or would his hubris once again lead him astray? Only time would tell.

The following morning, as Holmes and Watson were to depart on another ill-conceived adventure, I hastily scribbled a note, outlining my findings and urging them to reconsider their course of action. I slipped the note beneath the door of 221B Baker

Street, hoping that Holmes would at least give it a cursory glance before dismissing it out of hand.

From my window, I spied Holmes as he discovered the note, picking it up with a disdainful sneer. Watson urged him to read it. Holmes begrudgingly obliged, his eyes scanning the page with a mixture of curiosity and annoyance.

"Well, Watson," Holmes declared dismissively, "it appears that someone has taken it upon themselves to do our job for us. A preposterous notion, I must say!"

Despite Holmes' scepticism, Watson could not hide his interest in the contents of the note. "Holmes," he ventured cautiously, "do you not think that we should at least look into these claims? It would be remiss of us to ignore such information."

Holmes sighed, clearly frustrated by Watson's insistence. "Very well, Watson," he acquiesced, "we shall postpone our excursion and investigate these allegations. But mark my words, this is nothing more than an elaborate hoax designed to distract us from the true matter at hand."

Unbeknownst to the intrepid duo of Holmes and Watson, I shadowed their every step as they embarked upon their investigation into the enigmatic Order of the Sable Serpent. Disguising myself as a street merchant, I was able to maintain a discreet distance whilst remaining privy to their conversations and deductions, relying on my expertise in lip reading when I was out of earshot.

Holmes, in his usual bombastic manner, began expounding upon his theories regarding the Order's involvement in the Chiswick murder. "I daresay, Watson, that we have stumbled upon a veritable cornucopia of deception and intrigue. The Order of the Sable Serpent is, without question, a most pernicious and insidious organisation, one that has undoubtedly cast a pall over the victim's untimely demise."

Watson enthusiastically nodded in agreement, his brow furrowed in consternation. "Indeed, Holmes, it is a most distressing state of affairs. One cannot help but wonder at the depths to which these individuals will sink in order to protect their own interests and conceal their dark motives."

As Holmes and Watson traversed the murky streets of London, they paid a visit to several disreputable establishments that they believed to be connected to the Order of the Sable Serpent. In one such den of iniquity, they conversed with a louche and furtive character who purported to have knowledge of the Order's activities.

"My good man," Holmes inquired with feigned nonchalance, "might you perchance be acquainted with the symbol of a serpent encircling an orb, a hallmark of a certain clandestine society?"

The informant, his eyes darting about suspiciously, responded in hushed tones, "Aye, I've seen the likes of it. The Order of the Sable Serpent, they call themselves. 'Tis said they wield great power and influence in the shadows, meddling in affairs best left undisturbed."

Holmes pressed the man for further information, but it was clear that he had reached the limit of his knowledge – or was simply unwilling to divulge more. Frustrated but undeterred, the detective duo continued their pursuit of the truth, following a tangled web of leads and rumours that wound through the darkest corners of the city.

Throughout their investigation, I could not help but observe the many missteps and erroneous conclusions that Holmes, in his imbecilic state, made at every turn. It was both tragic and comical to witness a mind, thought by many readers of The Strand as brilliant, operating at such a farcical level of incompetence.

As dusk fell, the setting sun casting an eerie gloom upon the streets, I maintained my vigil, curious to see if Holmes and

Watson would ever manage to extricate themselves from the morass of their own making and arrive at the truth that lay hidden in plain sight.

As the twilight deepened and the gas lamps flickered to life, casting their dim, pallid glow upon the cobbled streets, Holmes and Watson found themselves in the heart of London's most disreputable quarter. It was here, amidst the squalor and degradation, that they hoped to uncover the secrets of the Order of the Sable Serpent.

They entered a dilapidated tavern, its sagging timbers and grimy windows lending the establishment an air of decay and despair. Undeterred by the foreboding atmosphere, the intrepid pair approached the barkeep, a man of prodigious girth and dubious countenance.

Holmes, affecting an air of casual insouciance, addressed the man with affected cordiality. "Good evening, sir! We find ourselves in need of both sustenance and information. Might you be so kind as to direct us to a suitable source for the latter, perchance in connection with the Order of the Sable Serpent?"

The barkeep eyed them warily, his corpulent jowls quivering with ill-concealed suspicion. "You're asking after matters best left unspoken, gents," he rumbled ominously, his voice like the distant rumble of thunder. "Prying into such affairs can have dire consequences, mark my words."

Watson, sensing the gravity of the situation, attempted to mollify the man with a placatory gesture. "We have no desire to court danger, good sir, merely to satisfy our curiosity and shed light upon a matter of some urgency."

The barkeep's steely gaze softened ever so slightly, and he gestured toward a shadowy corner of the tavern, where a solitary figure sat hunched over a tankard of ale. "Yonder sits a man who may be able to assist you, if you're so inclined," he intoned gravely. "But take heed: the path you tread is fraught with peril, and not all who venture upon it emerge unscathed."

With expressions of solemn gratitude, Holmes and Watson made their way to the designated corner and initiated a conversation with the enigmatic figure. His face was obscured by a wide-brimmed hat, and his voice was low, little more than a rasping whisper.

As the mysterious stranger spun a tale of clandestine meetings, nefarious plots, and unspeakable acts committed in the name of the Order, I could not help but marvel at the audacity of Holmes' misguided deductions and his obstinate refusal to acknowledge the evidence that lay before him.

As Holmes and Watson continued their conversation with the enigmatic stranger, I discerned the man's countenance becoming progressively more animated, his rasping whispers intensifying to an urgent sotto voce. The revelation of the Order of the Sable Serpent's inner workings was unspooling like a morass of intrigue and chicanery, the miasma of which appeared to be ensnaring the intrepid pair in its insidious tendrils.

"Hidden within their gaff," the stranger confided, his voice tremulous with emotion, "there's this book, right, chock-full of mystic know-how, so bally strange it gives Mother Nature the hump. The Order's looking to learn its rotten power for their own dodgy deals, not caring a monkey's about the bloody disaster that might hit our manor."

Holmes, his countenance a study in incredulity, furrowed his brow and queried the stranger. "Pray tell, good sir, what manner of calamity do you portend? Are we to believe that this obscure fraternity wields the power to unleash devastation upon our unsuspecting populace?"

The stranger, his tongue loosened with a fist full of sovereigns and with an air of solemn gravitas, nodded in assent. "Indeed, sir.

This bunch of geezers, if left to their own devices, could put us in a world of pain. Bringing down toff and pauper alike."

Watson, his eyes wide with consternation, interjected. "Surely, there must be some means by which we can thwart their malefic intent. Is there not some stratagem we might employ to extricate ourselves from this quagmire of villainy?"

The stranger leaned in closer, his voice barely audible. "There's only one way to make 'ead or tail of this mess, ain't it? You've got to sneak into the heart of the Order, worm your way into their most closely kept mysteries, and grab that blasted book from their mitts afore its wicked powers are fully let loose. And to do that, you'll need a passphrase I've heard them utter at the door."

After a further exchange of sovereigns and sideways glances, our enigmatic friend whispered *"fraga et crepito."* Holmes, with a determined glint in his eye, rose to his feet. "Thank you, sir, we shall undertake this perilous endeavour, heedless of the dangers that may befall us in pursuit of the greater good. Come, Watson, we have not a moment to lose."

As the benighted duo hastened from the tavern, I followed closely behind, my vigilance ensuring that I remained unseen. Notwithstanding Holmes' customary ineptitude, it seemed as though progress towards our mutual goal had been achieved.

As Holmes and Watson traversed the dimly lit streets of London, their path illuminated by flickering gas lamps casting eerie shadows upon the cobblestones, they engaged in fervent discourse regarding their newly acquired knowledge of the Order of the Sable Serpent.

Holmes, his inquisitive nature piqued, waxed lyrical on the purportedly nefarious actions of the secret society, his haphazard conjectures veering perilously close to the realm of absurdity. "Watson, I daresay this insidious Order may have tentacles extending into the upper echelons of our government, their influence perhaps reaching as far as the Royal Family itself! The game is afoot!"

Watson offered a more measured assessment of the situation. "Holmes, we must be cautious not to let our imaginations run amok. While the Order may indeed be a force to be reckoned with, we must first ascertain the veracity of the information we have received. We do not know if that shadowy figure can be trusted. Let us not forget our primary objective: to uncover the truth behind the grisly murder in Chiswick."

Holmes, momentarily chastened by his friend's admonition, nodded his agreement. "Quite so, Watson. Your sagacious counsel is, as ever, most invaluable. We must proceed with both circumspection and diligence in our investigation of this shadowy organisation."

They continued to traverse the oppressively dark streets of the metropolis, their conversation meandering through various topics related to the case at hand. Occasionally, Holmes would expound upon some fanciful theory or another, his overactive imagination leading him astray. Each time, however, Watson's prudent guidance would redirect him towards a more plausible line of inquiry, preventing their investigation from devolving into utter farce.

As I stealthily trailed the pair, I was acutely aware that it would be incumbent upon me to intervene should their investigation become irretrievably mired in Holmes' misguided deductions. Thus, I maintained my hidden observation, prepared to act as the unseen guardian angel of their endeavours, ensuring that the truth would ultimately be brought to light.

It was a curious dance we performed, Holmes and Watson blundering their way through the twisted alleys of mystery and intrigue, while I, the silent observer, remained ever vigilant, poised to step in and salvage their investigation from the precipice of folly. In this bizarre tale of buffoonery and brilliance, it was the unassuming figure of Dr Watson who emerged as the true hero, his steadfast rationality providing the anchor necessary to keep the great detective's flights of fancy from spiralling into utter absurdity.

From my concealed vantage point, I observed Holmes and Watson as they approached a dilapidated edifice, its crumbling façade all but obscured by the encroaching tendrils of ivy that clung tenaciously to its aged brickwork. The once-grand structure bore the unmistakable air of decay, a testament to the passage of time and the relentless march of progress that had left it behind.

As they drew nearer, Holmes noted with considerable interest the presence of the very symbol we had been investigating, etched discreetly upon the ancient oak door that served as the entrance to the enigmatic abode. The detective could barely contain his excitement, and his voice took on an animated cadence as he addressed Watson.

"Ah, Watson, behold! The very sigil we have been seeking, emblazoned upon yonder portal! We have, beyond a shadow of a doubt, stumbled upon the very lair of the Order of the Sable Serpent!"

Watson, exhibiting a more cautious disposition, counselled restraint. "Holmes, while this may indeed be the headquarters of the Order, we must tread carefully. We know not what awaits us within these foreboding walls."

Undeterred, Holmes strode confidently to the door, rapping upon its time-worn surface with a theatrical flourish. The sound of his knocking echoed ominously through the still night air, and a palpable sense of anticipation settled over the scene.

After what seemed an interminable wait, the door creaked slowly open, revealing a figure swathed in shadows. The hooded sentinel peered out at the intrepid duo, his visage all but concealed by the voluminous folds of his cloak.

In a display of unmitigated frivolity, Holmes attempted to ingratiate himself with the mysterious figure, employing an ill-advised and poorly executed attempt at flattery. "Greetings, good sir! I must say, your organisation has chosen a most impressive and atmospheric domicile. Would you be so kind as to grant us entry, that we might learn more of your estimable Order?"

The cloaked figure, evidently unimpressed with Holmes' obsequiousness, merely raised an eyebrow and muttered an unintelligible question about a passphrase. Holmes, ever the imbecile, endeavoured to mimic the passphrase provided by the mysterious stranger in the wide-brimmed hat, mangling the words beyond recognition.

"*Froga et crepato.*" After a long pause, the cloaked figure simply shrugged his shoulders and made to close the door in their face. Watson, stepping in to save the situation from devolving into complete farce, cleared his throat and repeated the passphrase "*fraga et crepito*" with impeccable enunciation. The hooded figure, placated by Watson's display of competence, grudgingly granted them entry, the heavy oak door swinging open to reveal the shadowy recesses of the Order's sanctum.

As they crossed the threshold, I remained concealed in the shadows, poised to follow them into the heart of darkness, ever watchful for the potential pitfalls and perils that lay in wait.

Gaining access to the edifice through a narrow open window, I adorned a long cloak draped over a rusty hook and stealthily trailed Holmes and Watson, ensuring that I remained hidden from view as they navigated by torchlight the shadowy corridors of the Order's stronghold. The air within the ancient building was thick with a palpable sense of secrecy, as if the very walls themselves were privy to untold mysteries and clandestine machinations.

As the intrepid duo proceeded, they encountered a small gathering of Order members, their faces obscured by the customary hooded cloaks. They spoke in hushed tones; their voices barely audible even to my keen ears. Holmes, in his usual manner, attempted to engage the group in light conversation, his inquiries woefully transparent and lacking in subtlety.

"Ah, esteemed members of the Order of the Sable Serpent, I presume? My associate and I were hoping to learn more about your esteemed society. Perhaps join if we like what we hear. Do we have to purchase our own cloaks? Might you elucidate upon the nature of your organisation and its objectives?"

The hooded figures exchanged wary glances; their suspicions evidently aroused by Holmes' artless line of questioning. It was Watson, once again, who managed to salvage the situation, his innate tact and diplomacy coming to the fore.

"My colleague and I are merely scholars with a keen interest in esoteric societies, and we have been particularly intrigued by the lore surrounding your Order. We humbly seek a greater understanding of your noble purpose, that we might further our own intellectual pursuits."

The members of the Order, seemingly mollified by Watson's eloquent entreaty, acquiesced to their request for information. One of the hooded figures stepped forward and began to speak in a sonorous tone, the words flowing mellifluously from his lips.

"Our Order, founded in the annals of antiquity, is dedicated to the pursuit of knowledge and the preservation of ancient wisdom. We seek to maintain a balance between the forces of darkness and light, wielding our influence in the shadows to guide the course of human events."

Holmes, unable to contain his misguided enthusiasm, interjected boorishly. "And what of the murder in Chiswick? Is it not true that this grisly act was perpetrated by one of your own in an act of retribution?"

A palpable tension filled the room, the hooded figures bristling at Holmes' brazen accusation. It seemed that our heroes had ventured too far into dangerous territory, and I steeled myself, prepared to intervene should the situation escalate further.

It was at this critical juncture that a tall, imposing, hooded figure emerged from the shadows, his commanding presence serving to quell the mounting unease. "Enough!" the formidable figure bellowed and, after the echoes abated, removed his hood. To the astonishment of Holmes and Watson, the figure revealed himself to be none other than Mycroft Holmes.

"Gentlemen," Mycroft intoned gravely, "I must apologise for the discomposure my brother has inadvertently caused. I can assure you that the murder of our fellow member was not sanctioned by the Order of the Sable Serpent."

Holmes, momentarily dumbstruck by his brother's unexpected appearance, managed to stutter out a response. "M-Mycroft, what on earth are you doing here?"

"It is no coincidence, Sherlock, that our paths have crossed in this unanticipated manner. As the head of this illustrious Order, I have been closely monitoring the developments surrounding the murder of Frederick O'Dell, or as he was more recently known, Atticus Bromsgrove."

Watson, a voice of reason, interjected with a pertinent query. "Might you elucidate upon the precise nature of the connection between the deceased and the Order, Mr Holmes?"

Mycroft, his countenance solemn, acquiesced. "Brother O'Dell was once a respected member of our Order, until his indiscretions left him vulnerable to the evil scheme of a blackmailer, a rogue agent from the now dismantled Elysium Brotherhood; the very organisation which you helped tear down this very year! In an attempt to escape his tormentor, he sought refuge within a new name. But this was not enough to remain at liberty, and he was soon rediscovered, eventually tracked down and then brutally murdered by this evildoer."

From my concealed vantage point, I observed as the elder Holmes elucidated further. "Our Order, despite its clandestine nature, remains a bastion of integrity and honour. We do not condone murder or acts of vengeance. Our primary objective is to uphold the principles upon which our society was founded."

Holmes, for once, appeared humbled by his brother's words, as he stammered an apology. "Mycroft, I beg your pardon for my earlier impertinence. It seems I have much to learn about the workings of the Order and the complexities of this case."

Mycroft, ever the stoic elder brother, offered a curt nod of acceptance. "Indeed, Sherlock. Let this be a lesson in the importance of thorough investigation and the perils of jumping to hasty conclusions. Our own investigations into this unfortunate series of events yielded only this shortlist of recent applicants to join our Order, all possible miscreants behind the whole murderous episode. Your quarry will be sporting a small tattoo on the left hand, in the fashion of the Elysium Brotherhood sigil, a compulsory adornment when nestled in the ranks of that wretched organisation." Mycroft handed his younger sibling what I would later discover to be a typed list of five names and a facsimile of the sigil.

With the truth of the matter finally brought to light, Holmes and Watson were left to ponder the implications of their discoveries, their previous misconceptions laid to rest. As for myself, I continued to observe from the shadows, ever vigilant and ready to step in should my assistance be required.

With Holmes chastened and the gravity of the situation now apparent, it was left to the sensible Dr Watson to steer the course of their investigation. As the duo prepared to take their leave of the Order's headquarters, Watson took it upon himself to address Mycroft Holmes.

"Mr Holmes, we are much obliged for the illumination you have provided on this perplexing matter. Rest assured that we shall redouble our efforts to bring the malefactor to justice and restore the good name of the Order of the Sable Serpent."

Mycroft nodded gravely, acknowledging Watson's determination. "We shall be grateful for your assistance, Dr Watson. I trust that you will keep me apprised of any further developments."

With their departure imminent, Holmes, still visibly discomfited by his earlier ignominy, mumbled a farewell to his brother. "Good day, Mycroft. We shall endeavour to resolve this matter post-haste."

As the pair exited the dark chamber and stepped into the murky London streets, Watson wasted no time in addressing the need for a coherent plan of action. "Holmes, we must eschew any further precipitous assumptions and instead focus our energies on unearthing the truth behind this sordid affair. To that end, I propose that we return to Baker Street and formulate a meticulous strategy."

Holmes, his earlier bravado having evaporated in the face of his blunders, meekly acquiesced to Watson's proposal. "Indeed, Watson, your counsel is most astute. Let us retire to our lodgings and marshal our thoughts."

As the two companions boarded a waiting hansom cab and began their journey back to their sanctuary at 221B Baker Street, I maintained a discreet distance, eager to continue my observation of their efforts. In this instance, it was clear that the hapless Holmes owed a debt of gratitude to the steadfast Watson, whose perspicacity and composure had prevented their investigation from descending into utter farce.

Once ensconced in the familiar confines of their Baker Street lodgings, Holmes and Watson embarked upon the formidable task of devising a scheme to apprehend the villain responsible for the untimely demise of poor Atticus Bromsgrove. As I surreptitiously listened to their conversation from my discreet vantage point, it became clear that Holmes' enthusiasm was undiminished, despite his earlier humiliations.

"The first name on our list," began Holmes, his voice barely above a whisper, "is that of Reginald P. Harrington, a purveyor of fine antiquities and a known associate of the late Mr Bromsgrove. It is not beyond the realm of possibility that he may harbour some resentment towards our unfortunate victim, perhaps stemming from a business transaction gone awry."

"Next, we have Millicent Fothergill, a widow of considerable means, whose late husband was rumoured to have been involved in some manner of unscrupulous activity with Bromsgrove," continued Watson, his brow furrowed in concentration. "It is conceivable that she may have sought retribution for some perceived wrong committed against her family."

Holmes nodded sagely before proceeding to the third suspect. "Ah, Michael Beaumont, a solicitor of dubious repute. It is said that he possesses a proclivity for gambling and has been known to engage in less than honest dealings. A man of his ilk would not think twice about resorting to violence to settle his debts."

"Indeed," agreed Watson, moving on to the penultimate name. "Then we have Gwendolyn Standish, a young socialite who was rumoured to have been involved in a romantic liaison with Bromsgrove. Could a crime of passion be at the heart of this sordid affair?"

"And finally," concluded Holmes, his eyes narrowing as he read the last name on the list, "we have Algernon Haversham, a rival businessman whose enterprises have suffered greatly due to the success of Bromsgrove's ventures. A motive most pedestrian, but one which cannot be discounted."

The duo proceeded to debate the merits and shortcomings of each potential suspect, their voices growing more animated as they weighed the evidence before them. As I listened to their deliberations, I could not help but be struck by the absurdity of the situation: Sherlock Holmes, a man of singular ineptitude, was entrusted with solving a case of such gravity, while the truth of the matter lay tantalisingly within my grasp.

Yet, despite Holmes' myriad failings, it was impossible not to be captivated by the unrelenting zeal with which he pursued justice, even as his ludicrous theories and outlandish stratagems threatened to undermine his efforts at every turn.

"Watson, we shall employ the most elaborate subterfuge to ensnare our quarry!" Holmes declared with characteristic bombast. "I propose that we assume cunning disguises, the better to inveigle ourselves into the confidence of each name on Mycroft's list. In this manner, we shall unmask the dastardly perpetrator and bring them to justice!"

Watson, impatient and exhausted by this behaviour, attempted to inject a modicum of rationality into Holmes' outlandish scheme. "Holmes, while I concur with the principle of employing subterfuge, I fear that your penchant for the theatrical may serve to compromise our efforts. Perhaps it would be more prudent to adopt a subtler approach."

Holmes scoffed at Watson's suggestion, his hubris unabated. "Nonsense, Watson! It is only through the most audacious stratagems that we shall triumph in this endeavour. I shall assume a myriad of guises, from a wandering minstrel to a purveyor of exotic comestibles! Our quarry shall be none the wiser until we have them securely in our grasp!"

With a resigned sigh, Watson capitulated to Holmes' outlandish plan, though not without reservation. "Very well, Holmes, we shall proceed with your proposal. However, I must insist that we exercise caution in our machinations, lest our ruse be discovered, and our efforts thwarted."

Thus, the two intrepid investigators embarked upon a farcical campaign of deception, donning elaborate disguises, and adopting preposterous personas in their pursuit of the elusive killer. As I continued to observe their proceedings from afar, I could not help but marvel at the boundless enthusiasm of Sherlock Holmes, an imbecile who, against all odds, remained undeterred in his quest for justice.

Despite the many shortcomings of their plans, Holmes and Watson embarked upon their visits to the various suspects, each excursion resulting in more comical encounters than the last. I shadowed them from a discreet distance, observing their comical attempts at investigation.

Their first meeting with Reginald P. Harrington transpired in a most ludicrous fashion. Holmes, donning an absurd disguise as a wealthy art collector, managed to spill a pot of ink upon a priceless tapestry, rendering the object utterly valueless. This, of course, led to a swift and ignominious ejection from Harrington's residence, but only after Harrington was ruled out as a suspect.

Next, they visited Millicent Fothergill under the guise of insurance agents. During the interview, Holmes expounded at length about the importance of securing one's financial future, only to have Watson inadvertently reveal their true identities by addressing his companion by name during a moment of frustration. The widow, understandably incensed, ordered them off her property forthwith. Nevertheless, no tattoo was discovered on Mrs Fothergill's left hand.

The encounter with Michael Beaumont proved similarly fruitless. Holmes, posing as a potential client in need of legal counsel, became so thoroughly entangled in a web of lies and half-truths that he succeeded only in confusing himself, leaving Beaumont bemused and entirely unimplicated in the crime. Watson did manage to take a good look at Beaumont's left hand before being asked to take their leave. Alas, no tattoo.

Their visit to Gwendolyn Standish took an even more preposterous turn. Holmes, believing himself to be a master of flirtation and feminine wiles, attempted to engage the young socialite in a conversation laced with innuendo. Alas, his clumsy overtures only served to offend the lady, who promptly excused herself and retreated to the sanctuary of her boudoir. Once again, no tattoo.

Having exhausted all but the final name on their list, Holmes and Watson reconvened at Baker Street, their spirits dampened by their repeated failures. As I listened to their despondent musings from my vantage point, I could not help but be struck by the sheer ineptitude of the great detective, whose every effort seemed to yield naught but red herrings and wasted ventures.

Nevertheless, I remained hopeful that, through some stroke of fortune, the pair might yet stumble upon the truth and bring the elusive murderer to justice.

"Shall we visit the last name on the list, Holmes? It seems clear as day that this name is the likely culprit." Proposed Watson.

"He can wait! Instead, I propose that we take a stroll down to Simpson's on The Strand and engage in a hearty dinner of steak and kidney pudding. What say you, dear fellow?"

Always thinking of his stomach, Watson agrees. "That sounds like a capital idea, Holmes. There is nothing to match the delights of Simpson's suet-laden delights!"

And off they went, disappearing along Baker Street under gaslight, with a spring in their step.

Despite the abysmal track record of the renowned detective, I could not allow the final suspect to elude justice. I decided to seize the initiative and ventured forth to the residence of Algernon Haversham, the last name on Mycroft's list and the probable culprit.

As Holmes and Watson revelled in the culinary safety of Simpson's, I approached Haversham's town house under the cloak of darkness. Utilising my discreet and stealthy skills, I gained entry through a basement window and began to scour the premises for any incriminating evidence.

My exhaustive yet silent search of Algernon Haversham's elegant townhouse yielded results that surpassed even my most optimistic expectations. The residence itself was a tasteful embodiment of the Victorian aesthetic, with its red brick facade, ornate ironwork railings, and tall, narrow windows adorned with lace curtains. Inside, the high-ceilinged rooms were decorated with an eclectic mix of furnishings that spoke to Haversham's refined tastes and worldly travels.

As I stealthily moved through the house, I encountered a sumptuous library filled with leather-bound volumes, its walls adorned with paintings of sylvan landscapes and ancestral portraits. The air was heavy with the scent of pipe tobacco and aged paper, and the flickering light from the fireplace cast dancing shadows across the room. The soft ticks and muted gongs of grandfather clocks completed the picture. It was here that I found Haversham's stately writing desk, a masterpiece of carpentry with intricate carvings and brass fittings.

I examined the desk with the utmost care, my fingers tracing its contours in search of hidden compartments or concealed drawers. Drawing a blank, I turned to the wood panelling covering the entire wall. My diligence was eventually rewarded when I discovered a cleverly disguised panel, which, when pressed, revealed a secret cavity within the wall itself. Inside this hidden nook lay a trove of illicit correspondence and incriminating documents – a veritable library of blackmail material.

The cache of documents and papers that I had uncovered in Haversham's hidden compartment painted a chilling portrait of a man consumed by ambition and utterly devoid of conscience. Haversham was a meticulous record-keeper, preserving drafts of all his correspondence, which I then understood could be the making of his downfall. The most damning pieces of evidence were the letters penned in Haversham's own hand, each one revealing a facet of his twisted psyche and his role in the murder of Atticus Bromsgrove.

One such letter detailed Haversham's scheme to exploit O'Dell, as he was known at the time of writing, and his vulnerability resulting from his scandalous affair. He had surreptitiously obtained incriminating correspondence between O'Dell and his illicit lover, planning to use it to coerce O'Dell into relinquishing his position within the Order of the Sable Serpent. This would allow Haversham to join the Order and ascend the ranks to further consolidate his own power within the secret society, and then to tear it down from within, in vengeance for the calamitous end to his precious Elysium Brotherhood.

There was a gap in the correspondence, presumably whilst O'Dell 'disappeared' to emerge later as Atticus Bromsgrove. An assortment of correspondences in the cache revealed Haversham's attempts, and final success, in exposing Bromsgrove as O'Dell.

A subsequent missive described Haversham's growing frustration with Bromsgrove's refusal to submit to his blackmail attempts, even after being rediscovered. In a fit of rage and finality, Haversham had resolved to take more drastic measures, enlisting the help of a disreputable associate to carry out the terrible deed. The letter contained meticulous instructions on how to infiltrate Bromsgrove's home and carry out the murder, ensuring that the Order of the Serpent were framed for this deed, and no trace of the Brotherhood's involvement would be left behind.

A third letter written to a comrade in the Brotherhood, written shortly after the assassination, revealed Haversham's unbridled satisfaction with the outcome. He boasted of his cunning and ruthlessness, expressing his eagerness to reap the rewards of his carefully orchestrated plot. It was apparent that Haversham felt not a shred of remorse for his actions, nor any qualms about the depths to which he had sunk in pursuit of his ambitions.

Interspersed among the letters were various other pieces of blackmail material, targeting numerous members of the Order of the Sable Serpent. There were transcriptions of meetings, ledgers documenting illicit financial transactions, and annotated maps detailing the locations of secret gatherings. It seemed that Haversham had painstakingly amassed this collection of incriminating evidence to manipulate and control the Order's members for his own despicable purposes.

The link between the blackmail material and the Order of the Sable Serpent was unmistakable. Haversham had exploited the secrets and indiscretions of the Order's members to further his own ambitions, with the murder of Atticus Bromsgrove serving as the ultimate manifestation of his villainy. It was a chilling reminder of the lengths to which some individuals would go in their quest for power and control, and a testament to the dark underbelly of the seemingly genteel world of Victorian society.

With the crucial evidence securely in my possession, I sought out a suitable vantage point from which to observe the arrival of Holmes and Watson. I chose a secluded spot behind a towering mahogany bookcase, affording me an unobstructed view of the room while remaining shrouded in shadow.

As I hunkered down in my concealed position, I could not help but reflect upon the events that had led me to this pivotal moment. The investigation had been fraught with missteps and miscalculations, the majority of which could be attributed to the baffling incompetence of the esteemed Sherlock Holmes. And yet, despite his many blunders, I could not deny that his involvement had spurred me on to greater heights of analytical acumen and deductive prowess.

As I waited in the dimly lit library, the creaking floorboards and a ticking clock my only companions, I steeled myself for the confrontation that was sure to follow. The stage was set, the players assembled, and the final act of this sordid drama was about to commence.

As Holmes and the ever-dependable Watson arrived at Haversham's domicile, bellies full, I remained hidden, curious to observe their farcical attempt at confronting the culprit. The duo, eager with purpose, knocked upon the oaken door with an air of feigned confidence.

Algernon Haversham, a gentleman of distinguished appearance, cautiously opened the door, his countenance revealing a mixture of curiosity and annoyance. Holmes, assuming the role of an itinerant violinist, began a cacophonous rendition of a popular tune whilst Watson, masquerading as his beleaguered manager, attempted to engage Haversham in conversation.

With vigorous drawing of his bow, Holmes winked an eye several times at Watson, as if offering a predetermined cue, his thrusts coming close to tearing a hole in a priceless canvas Failing to understand any significance of the gesture, Watson continued in ignorance.

Their clumsy subterfuge did little to advance their cause, as Haversham's suspicion only increased with each passing moment. Despite the ludicrous nature of their approach, Watson, in a rare moment of clarity, managed to divert Haversham's attention by mentioning the recent demise of Atticus Bromsgrove.

Haversham's demeanour shifted suddenly, and his keen interest in the subject betrayed his culpability. As the conversation progressed, Holmes, still absorbed in his ill-conceived disguise, continued to display a staggering lack of perspicacity. Watson, on the other hand, cornered Haversham with a series of pointed questions.

In that moment of realisation, the verisimilitude of Haversham's purported innocence dissipated like the ephemeral mist of a London morn. He endeavoured, with an air of desperation, to extricate himself from the formidable snare that was tightening inexorably about him. His visage, once a mask of genteel composure, became contorted with the anguish of a man who perceives the encroaching shadow of retribution.

As Haversham cast about for some plausible excuse to absolve himself of culpability, I considered the opportune moment had arrived to introduce the incontrovertible evidence I had obtained in the course of my undercover investigations. Ensconced in the shadows, beyond the ken of the assembled company, I deftly propelled the incriminating documents, with a waft of the curtain, across the well-appointed drawing room floor.

The bungling Holmes, the imbecilic detective who had so repeatedly stumbled through this labyrinthine case, appeared momentarily nonplussed by this unexpected development. His eyes, which had hitherto been clouded by the stupor of his own self-importance, now gleamed with a spark of comprehension. Grasping the incriminating parchment, Holmes flourished it with a theatrical gesture, as though brandishing a flag of victory upon a hard-won battlefield.

"Behold, Mr Haversham," he declared with a flourish, "the damning evidence that irrevocably links you to the heinous crime of which we speak. These letters, penned by your own hand, betray your perfidy, and illuminate the sordid affair that has culminated in the untimely demise of poor Mr Bromsgrove."

Haversham, the colour draining from his countenance, seemed to wither beneath the scathing scrutiny of the detective's gaze. The room, filled with the weight of unspoken recriminations, seemed to close in upon the unfortunate man, ensnaring him within the web of his own making. His mouth worked in a futile effort to articulate some form of rebuttal, yet the words, like phantom whispers, eluded his grasp.

It was Watson, the steadfast and dependable companion to the inept Holmes, who broke the oppressive silence. "Mr Haversham," he intoned gravely, "it is clear that you are inextricably entwined in this sordid tale of deception and murder. We implore you, sir, to unburden your soul of this grievous weight and confess your part in these proceedings."

As the words left Watson's lips, the atmosphere within the room grew palpably tense. Haversham's visage underwent a profound transformation, his countenance contorting into a malevolent sneer that belied the desperation and fear that lay beneath. With startling alacrity, he produced a gleaming revolver from the recesses of his waistcoat, levelling the menacing weapon at the intrepid duo. Haversham's weapon-bearing hand was now clearly adorned with a tattoo of the Elysium Brotherhood's sigil.

"Gentlemen," Haversham snarled, his voice laced with venom, "I fear I must decline your importunate entreaty, for I have no intention of surrendering myself to the tender mercies of the law. You have meddled in matters that do not concern you, and now, you shall suffer the consequences of your unbridled curiosity!"

Holmes, undaunted by the impending peril that loomed before him, regarded Haversham with a cool, dispassionate gaze. "Mr Haversham," he said calmly, his voice a paragon of composure despite his evident blundering, "your bravado is commendable, albeit profoundly misguided. I beseech you to reconsider your present course of action, lest you further compound the already considerable litany of misdeeds that weigh upon your conscience."

Holmes' entreaty, however, served only to incense Haversham further, his visage now suffused with a maelstrom of fury and indignation. With a cry of inarticulate rage, levelled his revolver at the ill-equipped detective, brandished with a wild, unsteady hand.

Watson, sensing the imminent danger that threatened his hapless companion, sprang into action, his movements an awkward dance of desperate improvisation. He hurled a nearby inkwell at Haversham, the projectile arcing through the air in a graceful parabola before connecting with the miscreant's shoulder, sending ink splattering across the room in a chaotic miasma of blue-black. Haversham reeled, momentarily disoriented by the unexpected assault.

Seizing upon this fortuitous turn of events, Holmes stumbled forward, his hands grasping for the revolver that now dangled precariously from Haversham's weakened grip. The two adversaries grappled with one another in a display of ineptitude, their struggle more akin to a comical pantomime than a desperate battle for survival.

As the absurd contest of strength and determination raged on, Watson, despite his own lamentable deficiencies in the realm of physical combat, valiantly endeavoured to assist his beleaguered friend. He launched himself into the fray, his arms flailing wildly in a futile attempt to disarm the obstinate Haversham.

In the midst of the ludicrous mêlée, a stray elbow from the bumbling Watson connected with Haversham's jaw, eliciting a pained cry from the desperate man. The force of the blow caused the revolver to slip from Haversham's grasp, clattering to the floor with an ominous thud.

Holmes, perhaps more by happenstance than any semblance of skill or cunning, managed to seize the weapon, brandishing it with a tremulous hand as he struggled to regain his footing. Haversham, now bereft of his sole means of defence, glowered at the dishevelled detective, a venomous mixture of rage and defeat etched upon his features.

As Haversham's resolve crumbled beneath the inexorable pressure of truth, he finally capitulated, his confession spilling forth like water from a breached dam. The tale he recounted was one of treachery and vengeance, borne of a heart ensnared by the basest of human desires; power, greed and avarice. It was a story that would leave an indelible stain upon the reputation of all who had been touched by its malignant influence.

As Haversham's voice faltered, the enormity of his predicament seemed to weigh upon him with crushing force. His shoulders slumped, and his eyes, once filled with defiance, now shone with the bitter tears of remorse. It was a pitiable sight, yet one that spoke to the immutable power of justice.

Holmes, for all his buffoonery, appeared to bask in the reflected glory of this unexpected resolution, his vanity puffed up like the plumage of a preening peacock. Watson, the true unsung hero of this tragic narrative, merely cast a sad glance at the defeated Haversham before turning away in disgust.

As the constabulary arrived to apprehend the villainous cur, I remained hidden, knowing that my assistance had been instrumental in the resolution of the case. Holmes, ever the egotist, appeared to bask in the glory of his perceived success, blissfully unaware that the true credit belonged to those who had operated beyond his purview.

From my concealed vantage point, I observed as Lestrade approached Holmes and Watson, eager to learn the particulars of their recent success. Holmes wasted no time in launching into an ostentatious and wholly inaccurate recounting of the events leading to Haversham's apprehension.

"With consummate acuity and unparalleled sagacity, my dear Lestrade, I managed to penetrate the very heart of this conspiracy," Holmes began, entirely oblivious to the fact that his involvement had been, at best, tactical. "Utilising an intricate stratagem of subterfuge and disguise, Watson and I were able to ensnare the dastardly Haversham and expose his contemptible plot."

As Holmes continued his embellished narrative, I could not help but marvel at the degree to which he was willing to inflate his own importance. Watson, to his credit, appeared somewhat abashed by the outlandish account, but refrained from interrupting his comrade's performance.

Lestrade, perhaps accustomed to Holmes's penchant for self-aggrandisement, listened with a mixture of bemusement and scepticism, occasionally interjecting with questions designed to challenge the veracity of the detective's account. Holmes, however, remained unfazed by these inquiries, skilfully evading the inspector's pointed queries with a combination of obfuscation and misdirection.

As the conversation reached its conclusion, Holmes reiterated his belief that his unrivalled intellect and ingenuity had been the driving force behind the successful resolution of the case. Lestrade, either unwilling or unable to contest this assertion, reluctantly congratulated the detective on his supposed triumph.

With the official proceedings concluded, Holmes and Watson took their leave, returning to Baker Street, no doubt to celebrate their purported victory. I followed, satisfied with my own role in the affair, but cognisant of the fact that the true extent of my involvement would forever remain a secret, known only to myself.

From the seat of the hansom that tailed the hapless pair, I observed the weary duo's return to their lodgings, the evening's chill undoubtedly hastening their steps. The soft glow of lamplight heralded their arrival and illuminated their familiar silhouettes, ensconced within their sanctuary.

Holmes, with characteristic exuberance, flung open the door, no doubt eager to commence his embellished recital of their recent exploits. Watson, ever the faithful companion, followed close behind, weary yet complaisant, aware that his participation in the narrative was both necessary and inevitable. I quickly paid my driver and headed into the comfort of my own sitting room, in order to eavesdrop on their comical colloquy.

Upon entering their abode, the pair set about the customary preparations for an evening of relaxation and repose. Watson, with practiced efficiency, could be heard stoking the fire, coaxing the embers to life and casting a warm, comforting glow throughout the room. Holmes, meanwhile, attended to the matter of procuring suitable libations, no doubt selecting a fine bottle of port from their modest collection.

With the fire crackling merrily, their glasses filled to the brim with the rich, ruby liquid, and pipes filled with tobacco keenly appropriated from the Whitechapel tobacconist shop, Holmes and Watson settled into their respective armchairs, the former eager to commence his grandiloquent tale, the latter resigned to his role as captive audience.

"It was an affair most extraordinary, my dear Watson," Holmes began, his voice assuming the melodramatic tone so often reserved for such occasions. "A veritable tapestry of intrigue and villainy, woven from the darkest threads of human deceit and malevolence. But, as always, the keen light of reason and deduction pierced the shadows, revealing the truth hidden within.

"Our tale commences with the arrival of our esteemed colleague, Inspector Lestrade... are you writing this down Watson?... who sought our assistance in unravelling the labyrinthine mystery of the Chiswick murder. The unfortunate victim, a certain Atticus Bromsgrove, had been discovered in his residence, the life cruelly extinguished from his mortal frame in a most grisly fashion.

"As is our custom, we hastened to the scene of the crime, our minds eager to dissect the clues that lay in wait. Upon our arrival, I was immediately struck by the peculiarities of the environ: the curious mark upon the window ledge, the distinct absence of any signs of forced entry, and a peculiar odour that lingered in the air, redolent of a malefactor's perfidy.

"From the outset, it was evident that the motives behind the crime were far from mundane. Our investigations led us on a winding journey through the darkest recesses of human nature. I deduced that the unfortunate Mr Bromsgrove was embroiled in a scandal of the most sordid variety, one which had made him vulnerable to the machinations of a blackmailer. Even after changing his name from Frederick O'Dell, he was unable to escape his doom.

"Yet this was merely the opening salvo in a grander scheme, one that encompassed a secret society, the Order of the Sable Serpent, to which our victim was irrefutably linked. This clandestine organisation, shrouded in mystery, bore the very symbol I had discovered at the scene of the crime.

"Our enquiries soon led us to the headquarters of the Order, a place of shadows and whispers, where our presence was met with a palpable air of suspicion. Yet, by some divine providence or stroke of good fortune, we were granted an audience with the elusive master of the Order, none other than – oh Watson, Mycroft swore me to secrecy – ah yes, a Mr Moncroft Homer.

"Mycroft – ahem - Moncroft, in his capacity as head of the Order, was compelled by I to furnish us with a list of names, each one a potential suspect in the sinister plot that had unfolded. Each name held within it the promise of truth, yet also the potential for further obfuscation and misdirection.

"With great diligence, we traversed the length and breadth of the city, visiting each individual in turn. The journey was fraught with peril and frustration, as each name proved to be a veritable Pandora's box, unleashing upon us a torrent of false leads and red herrings. Yet we persevered, undeterred by the myriad obstacles that sought to impede our progress.

"At last, we arrived at the final name upon the list: Algernon Haversham. A cunning and malevolent figure, Haversham had succeeded in concealing his nefarious deeds behind a veneer of respectability. Yet we remained resolute, determined to pierce the veil of deception that enshrouded our quarry.

"Fortune smiled upon us, for it was then that we discovered through cunning and guile the incontrovertible evidence of Haversham's guilt. The game was afoot, and the stage was set for a confrontation of epic proportions.

"Whilst performing a pleasant melody on the violin, I espied the sigil of the Elysium Brotherhood upon Haversham's left hand, whereupon I offered you a clear signal, dear Watson, that we were to act. Without delay, I quickly disarmed the man, leaving you the simple task of ensnaring the demon himself.

"Confronted with the inescapable truth, Haversham's veneer of civility crumbled, revealing the monstrous visage that lurked beneath. After a brief but containable struggle, he confessed his crimes, his voice choked with the bitterness of defeat. Yet even in the face of certain retribution, he remained defiant, cursing our names as we delivered him into the hands of justice.

"And so, my dear Watson, we find ourselves here, our arduous journey at its end, the tangled web of deceit and villainy unravelled by our tireless pursuit of truth. Haversham's downfall serves as a testament to the unyielding power of reason and deduction, a shining beacon of hope in a world beset by darkness and malevolence."

Watson listened with rapt attention, his eyes wide with admiration and fountain pen scrawling furiously as Holmes recounted their extraordinary adventure. "Indeed, Holmes," he responded, his voice filled with wonder. "It is a tale that shall be remembered for generations to come. Your keen intellect and unerring intuition have once again prevailed over the forces of evil, and the world is safer for your efforts."

"Pray tell, shall this case find its way into the pages of the next edition of The Strand magazine?" inquired Holmes.

"Indeed, my dear friend," responded Watson.

Holmes raised his glass of port, his eyes reflecting the flickering glow of the fire. "To the pursuit of truth, my dear Watson," he declared, a hint of a smile playing upon his lips. "May we never falter in our quest to illuminate the shadows, and may our resolve remain unbroken in the face of adversity."

As the two friends raised their glasses in a toast to their shared triumph, the firelight danced upon the walls of the Baker Street residence, casting a warm and inviting glow upon the scene. Whilst Holmes continued his oration, I could not help but marvel at the sheer audacity of his fabrications. His distorted account bore little resemblance to the actual events, the truth of which was known only to myself. Yet Watson, perhaps out of loyalty or an unwillingness to confront his friend, refrained from challenging Holmes's version of the facts.

So it was that, as the night wore on and the fire dwindled to glowing coals, the duo continued their exchange, their conversation punctuated by the occasional clink of glasses and the soft murmur of approval from Watson. In the end, I could not help but feel a pang of sympathy for the loyal doctor, burdened as he was by the unenviable task of bearing witness to Holmes's unrelenting self-aggrandisement.

Epilogue

As the embers of the fire slowly faded, casting a dim glow over the Baker Street residence, I found myself contemplating my own role in the events that had unfolded. From my vantage point, I had observed and guided Holmes and Watson through the intricate web of deception and danger that had threatened to ensnare them. And yet, despite my best intentions, I had made mistakes that had nearly cost them dearly.

Reflecting on the elusive escape of rogue inventor Marcel Merquin caused the bitter sting of regret and pain welled up within me. Though I had played my part in the pursuit of justice with unwavering dedication, I could not help but be haunted by the inescapable knowledge that I had failed to apprehend this evildoer, leaving him free to continue his flagitious schemes unmolested. In the quiet solitude of my reflection, I came to the sobering realisation that the responsibility for rectifying this situation lay squarely upon my shoulders. I knew that one day in the not-so-distant future, I would be called upon to confront Merquin once more and bring his villainous machinations to a resolute and final end. It was a task that loomed ominously before me, but one that I would face with unwavering resolve, for I understood that the pursuit of justice is an eternal struggle, a battle waged in the shadows as well as the light, and I was determined to see it through to its ultimate conclusion, no matter the cost.

The stolen dossier affair also weighed heavily on my conscience. I had unwittingly handed the precious documents back into the hands of the treacherous Mr van de Velde, a fact that haunted me long after the incident had been resolved. It was a sobering reminder of, perhaps, my overconfidence, and certainly the limitations of my own abilities. The consequences of a single misstep in this delicate game of shadows we played could be dire. I wondered, then, if my continued involvement in their affairs was truly for the best.

In the quiet solitude of my room, I considered the possibility of stepping away from the lives of the bumbling detective and his faithful companion, leaving them to face the challenges that lay ahead without my watchful guidance. After all, my presence had not been without its costs, and I questioned whether my assistance had truly been a blessing or, in fact, a hindrance, given Holmes' hitherto outstanding reputation in the public eye.

But as I mulled over my decision, I found my thoughts drifting back to the countless moments of triumph and camaraderie I had shared with Holmes and Watson, albeit from a distance. The thrill of the chase, the satisfaction of solving the seemingly unsolvable, and the knowledge that our combined efforts had brought justice to those who sought to undermine the fabric of society – these were the experiences that bound me to them, and the thought of abandoning them seemed anathema to my very being.

As the shadows lengthened and the final vestiges of the fire's warmth began to fade, I came to a realisation. While it was true that my involvement had not been without its pitfalls, the successes we had shared far outweighed the failures. It was in those moments of victory that I knew that our collaboration, however unconventional, had the power to change the world for the better.

With renewed conviction, I resolved to continue my secret assistance to Holmes and Watson, guiding them through the trials and tribulations that awaited them in the shadows of London's streets. I knew that the road ahead would not be easy, and that we would undoubtedly face challenges that would test the very limits of our abilities. But, with steadfast determination and unwavering resolve, I believed that we could overcome any obstacle that stood in our way.

And so, as I sat in quiet contemplation, my heart swelling with a newfound sense of purpose, I was roused from my reverie by the sound of a carriage drawing to a halt outside 221B Baker Street. Another mystery beckoned, another adventure awaited, and I knew that, together, we would rise to meet whatever challenges lay ahead.

In that moment, I understood that my role in the lives of Holmes and Watson was not merely that of a hidden guide, but rather a guardian, a sentinel who watched over them from the shadows, guiding their steps and shielding them from harm. And although they would never know the truth of my existence, the knowledge that I was there, a silent partner in their pursuit of justice, was enough to sustain me in the face of the darkness that threatened to consume us all.

I turned my gaze towards the street below, my eyes following the silhouette of the new client as they made their way towards the familiar door of 221B. I knew that this was but the beginning of another chapter in the storied lives of Sherlock Holmes and Dr John Watson, and I felt a restored sense of purpose as I prepared to embark on this new journey with them.

As I watched the client disappear into the warm embrace of the Baker Street residence, I realised that the bond I shared with Holmes and Watson, though unspoken and unseen, was as strong and enduring as any forged in the fires of friendship and trust. And as I stood vigil over the lives and fates of these extraordinary men, in their own way, I knew that we were bound together by a common purpose, an unbreakable thread that connected our hearts and minds in the pursuit of truth and justice.

The night air was cool and crisp, the stars twinkling brightly overhead as I gazed out at the darkened streets below. It was a world fraught with danger and deceit, where shadows concealed the sinister machinations of those who sought to do harm. But within the walls of 221B Baker Street, a beacon of hope burned bright, casting its warm glow over the city and banishing the darkness that threatened to engulf it.

As the clock chimed the hour, signalling the beginning of a new day, I steeled myself for the challenges that lay ahead. I knew that the path before us would be fraught with peril and uncertainty, and that our resolve would be tested at every turn. But, with each new adventure, I grew more confident in our ability to stand together in the face of adversity, to triumph over the forces of evil that sought to undermine the very foundations of our society.

And with that, I knew that my decision to continue aiding Holmes and Watson was the right one. No matter the challenges we faced, or the foes we encountered, I would remain steadfast in my commitment to guiding and protecting them, ensuring that their light continued to shine brightly amidst the shadows of the night.

END

Printed in Great Britain
by Amazon